THIS CRAZY LOVE

Swoon Series

J.H. CROIX

Cover design by Najla Qamber Designs

Cover Photography: Wander Aguiar

Cover models: Kerry Smart & Megan Napolitan

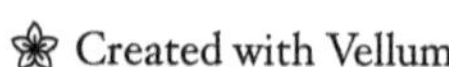 Created with Vellum

"Love is being stupid together." -Paul Valery

Sign up for my newsletter for information on new releases & get a FREE copy of one of my books!

http://jhcroixauthor.com/subscribe/

Follow me!
jhcroix@jhcroix.com
https://amazon.com/author/jhcroix
https://www.bookbub.com/authors/j-h-croix
https://www.facebook.com/jhcroix
https://www.instagram.com/jhcroix/

THIS CRAZY LOVE

Rule #1: Do *not* fall for your brother's best friend.

Rule # 2: *Absolutely* do *not* fall for your brother's best friend.

Rule # 3: Don't break the rules.

Shay

Jackson Stone is hot—like burn-down-buildings kind of hot. He's also my brother's best friend, and the memory of one kiss with him years ago still might get to me. Maybe. But, I am *not* looking for a second chance.

When I return to the small town of Stolen Hearts Valley, my life is a hot mess. I'm a few bucks shy of broke with nowhere else to go. My heart's battered and bruised, and when it comes to romance, the door is nailed shut.

But Jackson's the kind of man women ruin panties over. Oh, and he's my roommate. Talk about too close for comfort.

When I'm at my most vulnerable, he pulls that whole knight-in-shining-armor thing. What can I say? He's d*mn near impossible to resist.

Jackson

Shay Martin is my best friend's little sister. And she's so hot she nearly sets me on fire.

She's a walking complication, and I don't do complications. But I can't seem to stay away from her. It doesn't help that her bedroom is across the hall from mine.

Every look, every kiss, every touch nearly brings me to my knees. I can't keep my balance, much less think. Before I know it, I'll do *anything* for her. Complications be d*mned.

Chapter One

SHAY

I climbed out of my car, wincing slightly as the door squeaked when I tried to shut it. With a little extra push, it closed all the way. My car was a bit like me. It was hanging in there, but it was rough around the edges. I was rather attached to it. In fact, lately, I felt more kindly toward my car than myself.

Before my thoughts meandered too far down that path—a well-worn rut of recrimination and regret—my attention was snagged by a small horse galloping across the pasture in front of me. The horse was almost black with three white feet, as if it were missing a sock.

The horse angled to the side, just enough for me to see its tail flick behind it and notice it was a male. He kicked his back feet up in the air and turned to face the fence again. A white star stood out in the center of his forehead.

I was so absorbed in watching, I didn't quite notice what he was about to do until he came sailing over the fence in a beautiful jump, the kind that would've gotten him a ribbon in a show. Except we weren't in a show, and he'd just jumped out of the pasture. The horse came running straight for me, skidding to a stop before snorting and pawing at the ground.

Just as I was about to reach out, he spun around and dashed off again, kicking dirt in my face.

"Mischief!" a voice called.

Sputtering, I dragged my sleeve across my face. Looking ahead, I saw a man in the distance. A loud whistle followed his call. I wondered if that was Jackson Stone. I wasn't close enough to see from here. Whoever it was, he walked with an easy strength and grace along the fence line.

Taking a deep breath, I glanced around. I'd left before dawn this morning. A few hours of driving got me here just as the sun was rising behind the mountains. The famous blue haze over the Blue Ridge Mountains was shot through with gold from the sun's early rays.

My gaze made its way back to the horse I presumed to be Mischief. He slowed to a trot as the man approached him and then came to a stop, docilely lowering his head as the man slipped a halter on him. I watched as they turned toward me again. It was a minute or so before they reached me, but I recognized Jackson once he was close enough.

I once had a bit of a crush on Jackson, years back. With his shaggy brown curls and his piercing blue eyes, it was fair to say I was not the only girl who had a crush on him. I didn't think it was quite possible, but when he stopped in front of me, he was somehow more handsome than he had been before.

He wore scuffed leather boots with jeans, and a black T-shirt that didn't do much of anything to obscure the fact that he had a body to die for, all muscle and hard planes.

Stopping in front of me, his mouth curled into a slow smile. "How's it going, Shay?"

"Aside from getting dirt kicked in my face, I'm fine," I said with a laugh.

Jackson's smile turned sheepish with a shrug. "Sorry 'bout that. Mischief lives up to his name." He glanced to the horse in question, giving him an affectionate rub under his chin. "Mischief, this is Shay, and she's a friend. So, be nice. He doesn't listen too well," he added with a glance to me.

As if he understood, and to prove Jackson wrong, Mischief lifted his nose, gently nudging my shoulder with it. Despite teasing, I didn't really care about getting dirt kicked in my face. Dirt was the least of my worries. I lifted a hand and scratched between Mischief's ears, rewarded when he lowered his head and rubbed against my shoulder again.

When I looked back to Jackson, his blue gaze had darkened. A prickle ran up my spine, and I wondered if coming here was the smartest move. Problem was, it was my *only* move. I didn't have any other good options.

I forced a smile and replied, "Well, he listens to you."

A grin stretched across Jackson's face, and my belly executed a little flip. Oh my.

"He listens when he wants and that's about it. Let me get him back in the pasture, and I'll take you inside."

I watched as Jackson strolled across the parking area toward the fence Mischief had just cleared in an easy jump, as if it was nothing more than a minor nuisance. Opening the gate, Jackson slipped his halter off and patted him on the rump as Mischief flicked his tail before trotting off to join a cluster of horses in the far corner of the pasture.

"Need help carrying anything inside?" Jackson asked, as he stopped beside me.

His eyes traveled to my beat-up little hatchback. If he had an opinion about it, he stayed quiet. Once upon a time —which felt like forever ago at this point—I had a pretty good life.

I certainly had a car in better shape, and enough money to get by. Now, I didn't want to tell anyone how much I needed this place to stay right now. I had *maybe* fifty bucks left in my bank account. My little car was one of the few things that had seen me through both good and bad and was still chugging along, albeit a little banged up.

I watched Jackson's gaze coast over my car, hoping he didn't wonder about the dent just underneath the window in the driver's side door. A fist had left that behind. I didn't have the money to fix it and had learned insurance didn't cover people punching your car.

"Shay?" Jackson asked, his voice nudging me out of this ditch on memory lane, where I tended to get trapped.

"Oh right. I just have two bags," I replied quickly, finally springing into motion and striding over to my car.

Jackson insisted on carrying one of the bags, his fingers brushing mine and sending a hot little zing up my arm. I hadn't seen Jackson in five long years, but I'd never forgotten how handsome he was. Dear God, the man was swoonworthy and then some. Yet, I didn't recall reacting this way to him before, even if I'd crushed on him a little when I was younger and shared a single, wild kiss one night.

That zing startled me. I had written off desire, figuring my life would be better off without it. I also figured I was pretty much ruined for it. That's what a few years of bad sex tangled up with fear could do. It made me question everything about desire and my own judgment.

As I looked ahead to the farmhouse, I reminded myself, rather sternly, I needed this to work out. I needed a place to regroup, and this was it. Even *thinking* about the sudden, confusing attraction to my brother's best friend was a bad idea.

Chapter Two

JACKSON

Shay had a mere two bags with her. "I can get one," she said, her tone a little testy when I moved to take both bags. Shay had always liked to do things for herself, so I let it go and turned with the one I already had in hand.

Moments later, we were inside the house. I led her through the sprawling farmhouse kitchen, down the hall, and up the stairs, going straight to the bedroom Ash had determined would be Shay's.

After our father passed away a few years ago, my sister and I inherited the family farm. Years back, it had been a working farm for generations of our family. In the last decade or so before our father passed away, he had wound down the farming part of it, and dedicated his time to his horses and creating an animal rescue sanctuary. Before our mother died, he promised her someday he'd make the farm into a rescue.

Our father's death brought me home. In addition to the rescue program, we ran a small veterinary clinic, seeing as I had my license, but I hadn't put it to much use while I'd been overseas in the military. We'd also renovated two of the massive old barns into a high-end adventure lodge. We hosted a variety of guests throughout the year.

Ash was only here occasionally of late and was out of town now. She was one hundred percent on board with having Shay come stay here, so she made all the decisions about which room and so on.

Stopping by the door to the guestroom in question, I glanced back to Shay. "Right in here," I said, pausing once I stepped inside and set her bag on the floor in front of the dresser.

When I looked over at Shay again, my breath was nearly knocked out of me. The early morning sunlight hadn't done her justice. If I thought she was beautiful before, she was arresting now. Her dark blonde hair fell loosely around her shoulders. Her green eyes held mine as she looked at me, a hint of defiance entering her gaze.

Shay was on the short side and all curves. She wore fitted jeans and cowboy boots paired with a blouse. Even with her loose blouse, her breasts filled it, curves rising above the rounded neckline. Her lips were full and plump. She arched a brow as I looked at her.

"What?" she demanded.

I gave my head a little shake. "Not a thing. Ash will be thrilled to know you're here. You must've left early. Come on downstairs when you're ready. I'll take a quick shower and then I can show you around."

I walked through the door, trying to ignore the sizzle of electricity in the air when I passed by her. It wasn't until I caught her gaze out of the corner of my eye, and saw the vulnerability under the defiance, that I remembered all the reasons why she was here.

"I'll be down in a little bit. I just want to unpack," she said.

I'd been up for hours and on my back in the dirt,

changing the oil on one of the trucks. I needed a shower to clear my head as much as to get clean. I wondered if Shay was too close to my bedroom as I stepped through the doorway at an angle across the hallway. That was a problem for another day.

Chapter Three

SHAY

"Coffee?" Jackson asked, as soon as I stepped into the kitchen a bit later.

"Now?"

"In case you didn't notice, it's not even eight yet," he countered with a grin as he turned to look at me.

I had prepped myself for all kinds of things when my brother, Remy, suggested I come here to stay with Ash and Jackson. Ash had been my closest friend growing up, although we'd grown apart a bit in the last few years, and Remy and Jackson had been best friends all the way through college. They stayed in touch, even while Jackson was in the military and overseas and with Remy now living in Alaska.

Remy tended to have opinions about what I should do, and I usually ignored him. In this case though, I needed a change of pace like nobody's business. I was also more broke than I wanted Remy to know. The disaster of my life was something I was hoping to leave in the rearview mirror.

With Remy's suggestion and a phone call from Ash, I packed up what little I had and moved back to the Blue Ridge Mountains of North Carolina where I grew up. There had been absolutely nothing to keep me in Chapel Hill anymore, and piles of reasons to leave.

Of all the things I prepared myself to deal with when I arrived here, the sight of Jackson bare-chested with his jeans low on his hips was *not* on that list. He hadn't bothered with a shirt after his shower. My mouth went dry and heat bloomed through me.

Somehow, I'd conveniently forgotten how sinfully handsome Jackson was. With his damp brown curls, bright blue eyes, and a body made for sin, I was *not* ready to deal with my body's reaction to him.

I tried to take a deep breath, but my lungs weren't having it. With my pulse zipping along at a flat-out gallop and inconvenient desire spinning like fire in my veins, taking a deep breath appeared to be asking too much. I settled for a slow one, shallow and unsatisfying though it was. I nodded. "Coffee sounds great. I hope I didn't get here at a bad time."

Jackson's piercing blue gaze met mine. "Of course not."

"Okay," was about all I could say.

He held my gaze for what felt like too long, something flickering there. When he rested a hand on the counter, his fingers curling around the edge, my eyes tracked the subtle flex of his forearm, heat radiating through me at the sight. Blessedly, he turned away to start the coffee.

You cannot have a thing for Jackson. He's your brother's best friend, and he and Ash are doing you a favor. You need this place.

I thought I had my pulse under control until he turned back around, and I was abruptly reminded of the sight of his bare chest. Dear God. I felt as if I'd been cast into some twisted version of hell. This particular version involved me lusting after Jackson, quite inappropriately, when he had told my brother I could stay here as long as I needed. I was flat broke and an emotional disaster inside when it came to men.

"You hungry?" he asked.

I meant to say no, but my stomach had apparently developed its own voice and was able to understand human language. It promptly let out a loud rumble. In all honesty, I hadn't eaten since the granola bar I had late last night. I'd been anxious to get here today and had driven straight through once I woke in the early morning darkness, too restless and uneasy to sleep.

A slow grin stretched across his face. "I'll take that as a yes. Will scrambled eggs do?"

I swallowed and nodded, my mouth actually watering at the thought of food. "I can help. And I guess we should talk about, well, things like groceries. I can run to the store today," I offered, feeling awkward as I stood there in the middle of the kitchen.

"Ash stocked the fridge the day before yesterday before she left. You don't need to worry about it," Jackson replied, as he pulled some things out of the refrigerator. "Like I said, you're welcome to stay as long as you need. The bedrooms are empty. It's not gonna feel right if we're counting pennies. It might have been a few years, but you and Remy are family in every way it counts. When it's time to go shopping, whoever happens to take care of it is fine."

Suddenly, I wanted to cry. Between my body's abrupt and intense reaction to Jackson and finally arriving somewhere I hoped I could feel safe, I was so discombobulated I couldn't think clearly. The fear that had ruled my life for the last few years was hard to forget. I was about to cry over groceries and the simple offer of help from an old friend.

I was so accustomed to this emotional roller coaster I just rolled with it. Thank God my lungs worked this time. I took a deep, steadying breath and managed to stem the tide of tears threatening.

"Okay," I said softly.

Restless, I glanced around. Their kitchen was an old farmhouse style with counters lining three walls on one end and a massive island in the center. It had been updated since I'd last been here. There were new stainless steel appliances, bright blue curtains, and a round table with chairs across from the island.

Stools ran along one side of the island, and I slipped my hips onto one. Glancing over, I saw Jackson had pulled out eggs, a few red peppers, and cheese.

"How about I slice the peppers?"

"Sounds like a plan," Jackson replied.

He handed them over, along with a chopping knife and a cutting board, and I got to work. Within a matter of minutes, he had scrambled eggs with the peppers and cheese ready. I almost groaned when I took the first bite. I hadn't even noticed how hungry I was.

By the time we finished eating, the sun was fully up and the clock read eight thirty a.m. This lull during our meal felt downright domestic. Amidst my body's response to Jackson that just wouldn't quit, I was savoring the simplicity of the moment and how mundane it was.

Once upon a time, I had wished for excitement, a change of pace from the winding roads that brought me back to the Blue Ridge Mountains. No more. All I wanted was peace, quiet, and preferably boredom. I craved a routine where nothing out of the ordinary happened.

After I loaded the dishes into the dishwasher, I paused to look out the window over the sink. This farm was tucked into a valley in the mountains. I could see the far end of the pasture outside the window. Mischief stood at the edge of the herd, his head lifted as he looked at something in the distance.

My heart gave a hard thump. I could do this. Maybe, just maybe, I might be glad to be home in these mountains.

When Jackson left the table to go to the bathroom down the hallway, I figured I would head upstairs to shower. I didn't know what I was going to do for the rest of today, but I needed to start with a shower. I'd left before dawn this morning for the roughly four-hour drive here and hadn't even bothered to shower. Seeing as I wasn't even supposed to be staying in the empty condo where I snuck in late last night, I hadn't wanted to waste any time there.

As I stepped through the archway from the kitchen into the hall, I ran smack into Jackson.

"Oh!"

When I collided with him, my body felt as if it had been shocked with a live wire. I needed to move away, but for some reason I couldn't do it quick enough. For just a moment, maybe even seconds, I stood there frozen, right where his arms had come around to steady me when I stumbled at the impact.

Let's face it, running into Jackson *was* an impact. He was basically a wall of muscle. And he was warm and alive under my palm where it landed over his heartbeat. When I looked up, I almost wondered if I saw desire in his eyes, his blue gaze darkening.

Just as I became aware of the hard and rapid beat of his heart under my palm, I gathered myself together enough to step away. Tangling within this oh-so-inconvenient desire for Jackson was this urge to wrap myself in his strength.

Jackson was a good man. I knew that, without a doubt. He was not the kind of man to ever use his strength against a woman.

I had completely underestimated how much I craved being held. I knew my cheeks were flaming red when I looked up at him. He was quiet, his eyes searching my face. I wished I knew how to read his expression, but I had far too many doubts about my ability to perceive anyone accurately anymore.

With another one of his slow smiles, he winked. "Slow down."

"Um, okay," I muttered and hurried past him, practically running up the stairs.

I loved the charm of this old house, with its wide plank glossy hardwood floors, its tall ceilings, and windows deep enough for me to stand in. Yet, I promptly discovered one drawback. I wasn't a spoiled girl, but I wouldn't have minded having a bathroom right off my bedroom. As it was, I had stripped down to nothing before it occurred to me I needed to walk down the hallway to get to the bathroom.

Glancing out my window, I saw Jackson ambling toward the pasture as Mischief trotted to meet him at the gate. Clearly, he would be busy with something for a little bit. I grabbed a towel from the tidy stack on the dresser and wrapped it around me before running down the hallway with my bag of toiletries.

After a steamy shower, I felt half human and convinced I could get my body's runaway response to Jackson under control. With a deep breath, I tucked the towel under my arms and peeked out the doorway. Once I was sure the coast was clear, I stepped out.

It so happened my bedroom was at the far end of the long hallway from the bathroom. I tiptoed quickly down the hall. Just when I thought I was in the clear, the door at an angle across from my bedroom opened. I nearly jumped out of my skin and dropped my towel on the floor.

Chapter Four

JACKSON

Shay stood in front of me. Naked. With the fluffy white towel in a rumple at her feet, every inch of her was bared to me. Her skin was flushed all over, with her golden hair damp and slicked back away from her face.

I couldn't fucking help it. I mean, my God, I don't think any straight man could have kept from taking a nice long look at Shay. Her breasts were plump and full, her nipples a deep dusky pink and tightening under my gaze. My eyes tracked the dip at her waist and the lush curve where her hips flared out. I managed to force my eyes up, although my cock practically stood up and waved at her.

She gasped and leaned forward, snatching her towel off the floor and flinging it around her body. "Sorry!"

I wanted to tell her there was absolutely nothing for her to be sorry about, but I thought perhaps that wasn't the right thing to say just now. When my eyes met hers, and I saw her cheeks flushed pink, the urge to kiss her was so strong, I had to order myself not to.

"I have to get dressed," she murmured, dashing past me, the door to her bedroom slamming behind her.

My hands literally itched to reach for the doorknob and open it. Apparently, I may not have been able to control my cock, which was so hard I could feel my zipper against it, but I could keep my hands to myself. Thank fuck.

I hadn't even remembered why I was in the hallway. Turning, I walked back into my bedroom. Oh right, I meant to go downstairs and get another cup of coffee. It wasn't reasonable, but I decided against it. I needed to get a handle on Shay being here.

Even though I'd only showered an hour ago, I took a cold shower and went downstairs. After getting that coffee, I headed to my office, which was upstairs in one of our renovated barns. This farm had been in my family for generations.

My father had passed away two years ago. To this day, I wasn't quite so sure he hadn't simply died of grief. The medical report said he had a heart attack. Yet, he never bounced back after my mother passed unexpectedly from ovarian cancer that was caught way too late, only a year prior to his death.

The property had been transformed from its working farm days with our new ventures. Since we had the space, we were one of the few rescue programs in the area for larger animals, such as horses, goats, and the like. That's how we ended up with Mischief.

At the moment, we had eight horses, four dogs, five cats, seven chickens, two roosters, a few rabbits, a pair of goats, a mini pig that turned out not to be mini, and an actual mini pig. The pigs in question were both affectionate, and the small one, Squeaky, loved to follow people around. The not-so-mini pig was gigantic at this point. Gloria was everyone's best friend, and meandered around visiting whomever she came across.

Pushing through the barn doors, I turned down the side hallway and jogged up the stairs. This was a newer barn.

We'd renovated the two older barns roughly a quarter mile away, through some trees and over a small rise, into the adventure lodge with guestrooms and a large restaurant in the lower portion of one of the barns. A massive kitchen served guests as well as our staff. We ran tours for hiking and various wilderness adventures in the mountains surrounding the area.

There were a few small cabins scattered in the trees. Some were for guests and others housed staff who lived on-site, which was almost everyone who worked here. We had a staff of about fifteen between everything associated with the lodge, and running the rescue and office. Ash and I were both first responders and veterinarians, so that was something else layered onto the rest. Suffice it to say, we were busy. But our father's vision to transform the farm had come to fruition.

It was safe to say I was never bored. I was also rarely distracted. Yet, today when I sat down at my desk to take stock of just what the hell I needed to do, my mind kept spinning back to the sight of Shay bare in front of me.

When Remy asked me if she could come here, of course I said yes. I hadn't even hesitated. I knew Shay had been through fucking hell. Plus, she was a friend—one of Ash's closest friends and Remy's younger sister.

I recalled thinking she was beautiful the last time I'd seen her, but then, I had successfully put her in the best-friend's-younger-sister-don't-you-dare-touch category. That, despite one crazy kiss years back, when she was in college. Somehow, I'd managed to shove that out of my mind and consider it a fluke. Now, I was quite sure that was going to be impossible.

My office phone rang on my desk, effectively nudging me into awareness. This line only rang for two reasons—outside calls for the vet clinic, or internal calls from anywhere on the sprawling lodge.

Dani Love's name flashed on the screen. Dani ran the kitchen and helped out with managing guest reservations online. I didn't know what we'd do without her. Tapping the speaker button, I said, "Hey, Dani, what's up?"

"Hey, boss, we had a problem with an order of cheese. I've gotta head into town. Need anything else?" she asked.

Town, in this case, was Asheville, a good forty-five minutes away. "No, I think I'm all set at the house. Ash went a little nuts shopping for Shay last week before she left."

"Oh, that's right. Your friend is here. Are you going to bring her down to meet me today? You better," Dani ordered.

I'd been in such a rush to leave the house, it hadn't crossed my mind I would have normally planned to bring Shay around and introduce her to everyone this morning. I needed to get a grip and behave as I usually would. As unsettled as I was by my intense reaction to Shay, I needed to get it under control. Stat.

"Oh yeah, I need to take care of a few things here at the office, and then I'll go get her. When do you think you'll be back from town?"

"Before lunch."

"Gotcha. How about I aim for lunchtime?"

"Perfect. I'll make her something amazing."

After I got off the phone with Dani, I threw myself into work for the rest of the morning. Fortunately, I had a few regularly scheduled appointments, including one with a geriatric diabetic dog, a rather rotund little black-and-white sweetheart of a mutt named Emma.

"Well, Emma, you did great today," I said, scratching behind one of her ears as her tail thumped happily on the stainless steel examination table.

Her owner, Nana Tuttle, pretty much matched her dog. She was round and sweet with her once black hair mostly silver now.

"Nana, you're managing her diabetes just fine," I commented, glancing to her. Emma's tail thumped again, her gaze expectant. "Oh, that's right, you're waiting for a treat." Turning, I fished a small treat out of the jar we kept on the counter.

Chapter Five

JACKSON

After Emma left with Nana, I glanced down at my watch, realizing it was time for lunch. Somehow, by force of will, I had temporarily stopped my mind's replay of Shay naked in the hallway this morning. As soon as I became aware of that, the full vision in all its glory flashed in my mind. Fuck me. It was *not* smart to lust after Shay. She was my best friend's little sister. She was also here because she had escaped a disastrous relationship that, according to the news and Remy, had almost gotten her killed.

I sobered. It was hard to reconcile what happened to her with the Shay I had known growing up. Shay and Ash were the same age. At twenty-eight, she was five years younger than me. I recalled her as full of heart and saucy. Like Ash, she picked up strays in her life, left and right. Her ex, Clint Glover, the son of a high-profile politician in North Carolina, however, hadn't been a stray. He'd most definitely capitalized on her tendency to think the best of others, to give everyone a chance.

Shay's feisty personality was like sunshine and steel spun together. I'd seen a few hints of that since she arrived this morning, but I wondered how much life had changed her. I knew more than I wished about how events could shape a person and send a life skidding onto a different path. With a mental shake, I powered down my computer and turned to leave.

When I stepped outside the barn, Shay was leaning against the fence with Mischief nuzzling her shoulder. Since I'd last seen her, with nothing more than a towel to cover her glorious curves, she'd changed into a pair of fitted jeans that did little to disguise her glorious body. A loose blouse swirled around her hips. The sun was high in the sky now, her dark blonde hair sparkling under its bright rays.

As I walked toward her, my cock stirred. What had once been nothing more than a passing appreciation of Shay's beauty had turned into full-blown lust.

For now, it would be just Shay and me in the house with Ash gone for now. I hadn't even considered this could be a problem when Ash and then Remy asked if Shay could stay here. If I could get my body to behave, it wouldn't be.

I crossed the gravel area between the barn and the house. Shay turned when I got close, a guarded look in her eyes. "Oh, it's you," she said.

"Hey, Shay," I replied, doing my damnedest to ignore the way my pulse lunged. Shay was all cool green eyes, high cheekbones, and full lips. With her slightly crooked mouth, her slow smile was endearing. "I came to find you. I want to take you around to meet everybody at the lodge. There're quite a few of us. Dani wants to feed you lunch, so I figured we could start there."

"I'd love to meet everyone. I'm just glad y'all invited me to stay."

"You're like family, Shay," I stated, a repeat of what I said earlier this morning.

Uncertain what else to say, I turned and started walking in the direction of the lodge, roughly a quarter mile from where we were now. Shay caught up to me quickly, and immediately asked, "How long will Ash be away? She said she was traveling, but not much else."

"She's chasing after some guy she met on the rodeo circuit," I explained, striving to keep my tone level. I thought the guy was an ass.

"Ah, she mentioned some guy she met when she was playing somewhere out in Texas."

"Yup, that's the one." Ash had spent most summers traveling to play small music venues. Her guitar was an extension of her body, and her voice was pure heaven.

"So, what would you like me to do around here?" Shay asked.

"There's always something to do. With Ash gone right now, we could use the most help with the rescue. Seeing as you love animals, I figured you wouldn't mind. I can take you over there this afternoon and get you up to speed on the schedule. It's mostly feeding every morning and evening, and then coordinating with me on any who need some vet care. Other than that, it's staying on top of calls and emails about potential rescues and adoptions. We try to take every request, but here and there, we've got to hunt down better options. We can usually make do unless there are significant problems with aggression. Even then, we've got short-term solutions."

"I can certainly handle that. If you need any other help, just say the word."

We crested the small rise between the main house and barn compound, and the old barns that had been renovated into the adventure lodge came into view. My great-grandparents had found this beautiful piece of property nestled in the foothills of the Blue Ridge Mountains. It was tucked into a small valley, and the mountains rose around us. To me, these mountains felt as if they were cradling you. They were nothing like the massive mountains out West that towered above. These were intimate, filled with winding roads, small valleys, and nooks and crannies. Dense, fragrant greenery surrounded you in the spring and summer.

Shay stopped, her breath coming out in a little gasp. "I forgot how beautiful it was," she said reverently.

Glancing to her, my eyes landed on a fine scar, just along her hairline. I didn't want to think about why it was there. The moment I forced my eyes away, they snagged on her lips, and she glanced to me.

Fuck me. Shay Martin had a straight line to the pulse of my desire.

I had to clear my throat to speak. "It is. Come on, Dani'll be waiting," I said, perhaps too brusquely.

Although Shay had grown up in these mountains, I didn't know if she'd been back since her parents died. They had been killed by a tornado when they were on vacation. That had only been a few years ago. I knew she didn't visit much the year before they died, and knew now it was likely her ex who kept her from coming. Fury lashed at me thinking about that. Shay and Remy had been close to their parents. I recalled Remy's concern about Shay, but we hadn't known just how bad things were until it all blew up.

Shay was quiet as we followed the path through the trees. In a moment, two massive old barns came into view. They had been updated with bright blue steel roofing that stood out amidst the landscape. The old painted siding had been torn off and replaced with stained cedar.

The barn further away was exclusively for lodge guests. The entire upstairs and downstairs had been transformed into guest suites, every room offering a view of the mountains surrounding the area.

The closer barn had guestrooms upstairs, while the downstairs had been transformed into a restaurant with a large kitchen and area for staff. In the guest area, a large recreational room with a massive stone fireplace anchored the space with several areas for seating.

I hadn't called over to Dani, but I guessed she had

already rounded up the staff. She would want everyone to make sure to meet Shay. I paused on the stone walkway leading to the main door of the barn. "Just a heads-up, but you're probably going to be bombarded here. Sometimes it's a bit scattered, but I'm guessing today Dani's made sure everyone will be here."

Shay bit her lip, worrying it. I had to remind myself—yet again—not to let every little thing she did set my pulse to pounding. She was quiet, and I could practically see the thoughts tumbling through her mind. She took a small breath, that guarded look entering her eyes again.

"How much does everyone know about why I ended up here?"

I didn't know what I had expected her to ask, but it wasn't that. "Shay, I don't even have all the details, but it was in the news. Remy called me and said you could use a place to stay, but I haven't discussed it with anyone. I wouldn't worry about what anyone might know. Everybody here is good people. I promise."

I was speaking the truth. However, I knew she'd been to hell and back in the last year or so. With her ex having a high-profile father who tried to downplay his son's assault on Shay, it had been splashed all over the local and state news. The story had dragged on after her ex killed two people when he slammed into their car while driving drunk. The whole thing had been rehashed. While victims of sexual assault had their name protected in the news, that wasn't the case with straight-up assault. Again and again, Shay's name had popped up. I beat back the fury rising inside. I'd have loved fifteen minutes alone in a room with her ex. He wouldn't walk out after I was done.

Shay's mouth twisted to the side as she chewed on the corner of her lip. "Oh, okay."

"Is there something else I should know?" I asked.

Her eyes met mine. "No, no," she replied with a little shake of her head.

"All right then, come on in."

When we reached the doorway, I reflexively placed my hand on her lower back as I held the door for her, stepping inside with her. Although I knew without a doubt she had nothing to fear here, a sense of protectiveness cloaked itself around me. There were gaping holes in the details of what I knew about Shay and her ex, and that only made me feel more protective. Underneath the steel and sunshine that defined her, I sensed a hint of vulnerability that hadn't been there before.

Chapter Six

SHAY

With the heat of Jackson's palm on my back filtering through the thin cotton of my blouse, I was far too aware of his touch. My body practically spun like a top around him. I still hadn't fully recovered from this morning's accidental striptease in the hallway. I had several chats with myself, trying to talk my body into the fact that Jackson was just Jackson. I was hyperaware of his nearness and his touch. I hadn't experienced anything even remotely resembling desire in so long, I'd forgotten what it felt like.

My stern conversations with my body appeared to be all for naught. Because all I knew was I didn't want his hand to drop away from me, and I was disappointed when it did. A flash of longing pierced me.

"Hi, Shay!" a woman called as we stepped into a massive kitchen. It was clearly a working kitchen with a stainless steel table running through the center of the room, two double wide refrigerators against the back wall, along with two stainless steel sinks, and a giant oven and stove.

The woman in question dusted her hands on her apron and paused by one of the sinks to rinse her hands. She had wild, curly brown hair pulled into a ponytail high on her head. After she dried her hands, she hurried across the room and threw her arms around me. I reflexively hugged her back, unable to resist smiling as she stepped away. Her creamy skin was dusted with freckles and her green eyes were wide, crinkling at the corners with her smile.

"Um, hi," I said, uncertain what her name was.

"This is Dani," Jackson offered from my side.

"Nice to meet you, Dani," I added.

"We love having new people join us here," she said, her enthusiasm infectious. "Everyone's on their way for lunch and half of them already beat you here." She cast an accusing glare in Jackson's direction. "You're late."

Jackson shrugged nonchalantly. "Lost track of time. Nana brought Emma for her checkup, and we ran a little late."

I assumed he was talking about someone's pet. Just as I was about to ask, another voice called over. I glanced beyond Dani to see a large picnic style table, almost full of people.

Now, I understood Jackson's warning outside. Although he obviously knew a bit about the disaster of my life, thanks to my ex's family's high profile, he probably didn't know I was a tad rusty when it came to being social. I'd been isolated in ways I had never expected in the years I was with my ex.

So, yeah, this could've been too much. Yet, despite my body's haywire reaction to Jackson and feeling like a complete failure at life in general, I wasn't afraid. Not here. I trusted Jackson completely, so I knew anyone working for him was decent.

Within a few minutes, I was introduced to everyone and herded to the table. I found myself seated beside Jackson on a long bench seat. The table was crowded enough that every so often his thigh brushed against mine, sending a little jolt of electricity zinging through my body.

"So, I hear you're going to help with the rescue animals," Wade Ellis commented from across the table. Wade had rumpled brown hair, warm brown eyes, and an easygoing manner to him.

During the round of introductions, I learned he helped out running the outdoor hikes and was also a first responder like Jackson.

"I sure am," I replied.

"Had much experience with horses?" the man beside Wade asked. I thought his name was Lucas. With his almost black hair and deep green eyes, he was quite handsome. Handsome enough that I tried to will my body to react to him the way I reacted to Jackson, but less than nothing happened.

"I do, actually. I grew up riding horses. Ash and I were in school together, so I spent a bit of time here back when it was just a farm. It's been awhile because…" My words started to trail off because I suddenly wondered how much they knew about my too public past. I stumbled ahead. "I'm looking forward to it. I've missed being around horses."

Dani chimed in. "Hon, it's not just horses. There're dogs, cats, chickens, a pig, a mini pig, and some goats. I hope you don't mind the variety."

I shrugged. "Not at all. I love animals. I can't say I've ever dealt with pigs though."

Jackson's laugh rumbled low beside me. "Oh, you'll like Squeaky. She's probably the sweetest."

"Now, don't you say Gloria isn't the sweetest," Dawson Marsh teased. In the few minutes since I'd been seated, it was quite clear Dawson teased and flirted with anyone and anything. With his amber hair and silvery gray eyes, he had an outdoorsy, surfer vibe.

Despite how much he flirted, he was so easy to be with, it didn't set me on edge the way flirting usually did. After too long with an ex who attacked *me* when any man flirted with me in any way, I was a bit gun-shy.

"Squeaky and Gloria?" I asked.

"A giant pig and a mini pig, respectively. Squeaky came

with that name," Jackson explained with a grin. "A little girl who lives a few miles down the road found her on the side of the road. So, she came to us as Squeaky and she's still Squeaky. She, uh, squeaks and she loves people."

"Since Jackson left Gloria out, just know she's the queen around here," Dawson added with a wink.

Evie, whose last name I couldn't recall, chimed in. "Gloria is definitely the queen." She leaned forward to reach for a roll, brushing her glossy black hair off her shoulder when it slipped forward.

Jackson rolled his eyes. "Trust me, I know she's the queen. I fed her pancakes before sunrise today."

By the time lunch was over, I felt enveloped in the warm embrace of the friendly group. Ash had told me it was busy here, but I hadn't quite grasped just how busy. What had once been a farm was transformed into an upscale wilderness adventure lodge, veterinary clinic, and rescue program in one. Suffice it to say, there was a lot to do.

The work part seemed easy. In fact, all of it seemed easy. Except for my inconvenient response to Jackson. Sitting beside him at lunch with the potent force of his presence right there and the occasional brushes against him, I was hot and bothered all over.

To my mind's chagrin and my body's joy, I proceeded to spend the rest of the day with Jackson. He took me over and introduced me to all the animals in the rescue barn, reviewing their feeding schedules and more. He made sure I had his number in my phone to buzz him at any point if something came up. He left when he got an emergency call for his vet clinic. As he hurried away, he called back, suggesting I grab dinner over at the lodge.

At loose ends, I walked over and found Dani alone in the kitchen, kneading dough. She looked up with a bright smile when I stepped through the door. "Oh good! Did Jackson send you over for dinner?"

"He sure did. I hope it's okay," I offered as I glanced around.

"Of course it's okay. The rest of the crew went into town to Lost Deer," she said, referring to a longtime local bar in the area. Even though I hadn't lived in the area for over ten years, it had been a fixture since before I was born. "I'm working late on some baking prep, so I've got a small pizza I tossed in the oven. If you want, we can split it." She paused, her brow furrowing. "You're not a vegetarian, are you?"

When I shook my head, she grinned. "Good, because it's pepperoni."

I laughed. "I love pepperoni."

In the quiet kitchen, I helped Dani knead the dough and then we sat on stools by the table in the center of the room to enjoy her fresh pepperoni pizza with red wine. I felt like I was truly relaxing for the first time in years.

It wasn't that I hadn't had any friends to turn to after my life spun into disaster, but it has been hard to reach out because everyone knew what happened. It also happened too close to my parents' unexpected death, when a tornado plowed through the vacation home where they were staying while they slept in the darkness. To say the last few years had been hard didn't come close to describing just how difficult and painful it had been. The one touchstone in my life was my brother, Remy.

Yet, like everyone, Remy only knew the outlines of what happened. I didn't want to burden him with how much I'd endured.

It was nice to simply relax, enjoy some amazing pizza, and have a few glasses of wine. Dani was cheerful and welcoming. She was also quite nosy.

As nosy as she was, she was a fan of sharing information too. She readily answered any questions I had about Jackson.

The wine loosened my reserves, and I gave free rein to my curiosity about Jackson. "Seriously, I can't figure out why the hell no one has snapped that man up."

Dani rolled her eyes. "I know, right? It makes no sense whatsoever. He's like an older brother to me, so I feel nothing for him. But I know a sexy man when I see one, and Jackson is damn sexy as hell. Honestly, I think he's got a little thing for you," she said.

I almost spit my wine out. "What? I've been here a day. Pretty sure Jackson doesn't have a thing for me."

"Oh, I saw the way he looked at you. Plus, Ash said you two kissed once."

My cheeks were flaming, so hot I knew it was obvious. Dani's grin widened. "I see Ash wasn't making that up."

"It was just one kiss. Years ago. Anyway, I don't know why you think he has a thing for me. Trust me, I'm pretty sure he doesn't."

Dani shrugged. "Whatever. But if you ask me, Jackson could use a little love in his life. Ever since he came back from his time in the military, he hardly smiles."

Seeing as I hadn't spent much time with Jackson in years at this point, I didn't have much of a gauge to know how he was doing.

Whatever she saw in my eyes, Dani nodded, her gaze sobering. "He won't talk about it, but I know he saw some bad stuff. I mean, he was in Special Ops. I knew Jackson when we were little. He was a lot more easygoing then. I'm sure you knew, but practically every man in his family was military, so he voluntarily signed up and went off to Iraq. The only thing I really know is an IED went off and killed two of the guys in his unit. He got hit while he was trying to get them out. It was right at the end of his assignment, so they sent him home. He took a bullet in his side and a few bits of shrapnel from the IED. He hasn't been the same since he got back."

I hadn't heard any of this from Ash. But then, Ash and I hadn't talked much in the last few years. She had told me he'd been injured, but not these details. My heart wrenched to think of Jackson going through that.

"That's awful," I finally said.

Dani nodded. "Yeah, try pointing that out to Jackson. All he's got to say is he's alive."

What had started out as a teasing conversation had sobered quickly. Dani and I simply looked at each other for a moment before she sighed, blowing a puff of air to move a loose curl out of her eyes. "I didn't mean to be a downer."

"It's okay. I haven't seen Jackson in years, certainly not since that happened. I doubt he'll fill me in, so thank you."

Dani nodded and paused to sip her wine. "I like you," she said, after setting down her empty wineglass.

"Ditto," I said as I slipped off the stool, my reply reminding me of Remy. Whenever I told my brother I loved him, that's what he said.

I helped Dani clean up and then turned to look at her. "Need anything else before I head back to the house?" I asked.

"No, but I expect to see you for lunch tomorrow," she offered with a smile.

"I'll be there. Good night," I called as I turned to leave.

Chapter Seven

SHAY

Moonlight cast the landscape in a silvery glow along my short walk back to the farmhouse. Although the days were quite warm in the spring here, I had a jacket on because the air became cool once the sun slipped behind the mountains. I picked up my pace, shivering a little. The lights were glowing from the front hallway and the kitchen in the farmhouse windows as I approached, and I wondered if Jackson was home yet.

The mere thought of Jackson sent butterflies twirling in my belly. I opened the door quietly to let myself in, pausing to listen in the entryway. I sensed he was here, so I walked down the hallway, following the light into the kitchen.

As I stepped through the archway, my mouth went dry. Jackson stood at the counter, rinsing dishes and setting them one at a time in the small drying rack beside the sink. He hadn't bothered with a shirt. Sweet hell, his back was enough to send me into cardiac arrest. Heat rushed through me and my pulse took off like a rocket.

I simply stood there as he finished rinsing the dishes before he turned the faucet off. I hadn't even realized I was halfway across the kitchen until he turned around. His skin was burnished gold, the lines of his body defined and hard. I doubted Jackson had ever seen the inside of a gym. Yet, he was more fit than most men who spent hours there. His body was one born of raw, hard work. My eyes caught on a scattering of scars on his side, and I abruptly recalled Dani telling me he'd taken a bullet and been hit with shrapnel. My heart clenched. I shook my mind off that recollection.

He rested a hand on the counter, his gaze snagging mine. I couldn't move. I was frozen in place, caught in the air between us, which was shimmering with heat and electricity.

"How was dinner?" he asked.

"It was delicious, actually. Dani made pizza. It was just the two of us. Did you have anything to eat?"

He nodded. "Threw together a sandwich. Probably not as good as Dani's pizza though," he said with a grin.

My belly somersaulted. I needed to stop staring at his chest, but my eyes kept dropping. It was all too much—too much want, too much need, and too much confusion at the depth of my response to him.

I'd known Jackson since I was a little girl. I had never felt this way around him. We stood there, staring at each other. Just as I was wondering if I should find a way to gracefully run up the stairs, Jackson pushed away from the counter, taking a few strides and stopping in front of me.

My lungs seized. My heartbeat stuttered, and then lunged, pounding so hard I could feel it vibrating through every cell in my body. I remembered that one kiss. Vividly. I'd been in college in Chapel Hill. Jackson had come along to visit with Remy for a weekend.

Back then, Jackson had been young, handsome, and a flirt. Of course, I thought he was cute. Time had honed and tempered him, enhancing and sharpening his qualities—his rough-edged masculinity, his strength, and that lazy sensuality shimmering in his gaze.

My conversation with Dani flickered in the back of my

thoughts, and I wondered if those events had led to the slightly shuttered quality in his eyes now. His gaze wasn't quite as teasing as it once was. My heart squeezed.

As these thoughts spun through my mind like tumbleweeds blowing across the road, Jackson searched my face. I was a little tipsy from the wine I shared with Dani, probably not the wisest move on my part. Normally, my defenses would be on high alert. They almost always were.

I'd been tied up in knots and on edge for so long, being somewhere I could feel safe had me forgetting to keep my defenses up. I'd promised myself I wouldn't let my heart get hopeful again. I foolishly believed I could manage it.

All of my promises and foolish beliefs went up in smoke with Jackson standing in front of me. The young, teasing man I'd once shared a wild kiss with was *all* man now. He nearly set my body on fire. My knees were wobbly and my breath came in short little pants.

Without thinking, I reached out, tracing my fingertip along his jawline, savoring the prickle of the stubble.

"What are you doing, Shay?" Jackson asked, his low drawl rolling over me like honey.

My inhibitions, which I sorely needed about now, were long gone. I could feel the heat of him when I stepped even closer. The girl I'd once been, the girl who I had thought lost, came sauntering back inside of me. Before everything went wrong, I'd been rather brash and bold. I thought that part of me was long gone. Life teaches hard lessons sometimes. It can even steal bits and pieces of who you think you are.

Just now, I was surprised to learn another lesson. Parts of myself I thought lost had simply been buried. Not lost, not gone. That bold, brash girl was different now. I was older and wiser, and I certainly had bitterness swirled into my spine. Yet, in spite of that, for the first time in a long time, I felt playful and brave.

"What are you doing, Shay?" Jackson repeated.

My fingertips trailed down along his collarbone. His skin was warm to the touch. "Touching you," I said, a fizzy joy rising inside and spinning like glitter into the desire, caught fast in its shimmering force.

"I'm not so sure that's a good idea," he replied, his words almost careful.

Cocking my head to the side, I arched a brow. I knew I was pushing the limits here.

I might've been foolish and made incredibly disastrous decisions in my past, but I wasn't stupid. I knew Jackson wanted me, because I could feel it like a pulse between us. I could also see his arousal pressing against his jeans.

"Says who?" I countered.

I let my fingertips travel over the round curve of his shoulder and onto his chest, which was lightly dusted with hair. I could feel the steady, rapid beat of his heart under my palm.

He still didn't move away, and the air thickened around us. I was feeling downright wild now, bordering on reckless. Yet, all we were doing was standing in the kitchen.

I didn't know how to read his gaze. I knew I saw desire flickering there, and something else. In a way, I didn't care to read it. I was too caught up in this moment, almost giddy at the realization things I had written off—fierce need and desire—might actually be possible to experience.

Jackson muttered something, and then his hand was sliding into my hair and his mouth collided with mine. At first, it was a hot jolt, the point of contact fierce and rough. One hand glided down my back in a heated pass, while his other hand cupped my nape, his fingers teasing in my hair and sending hot shivers through me. His hold was both strong and gentle, all at once. Exactly what I needed.

When I sighed, his tongue slipped in between my lips. I hadn't forgotten my one kiss with Jackson before. That had been brief and hot, so jolting I hadn't known how to absorb it. This was different.

This was the most intense kiss I had ever experienced in my life. Slow, sensual strokes of his tongue, his mouth hot on mine, the catch of his teeth on my bottom lip, a teasing bite at the corner of my mouth. A molten, searching kiss that nearly undid me.

I was on fire, need scattering like sparks through me.

There was an odd sound, something resembling a squeak. The sound barely punctured the haze clouding my mind, but Jackson gentled our kiss before dusting a few soft kisses along my neck and lifting his head. I was stunned, almost surprised to find myself still standing.

There was that squeaking sound again. Suddenly, I realized what I'd just done and was mortified. And more turned on than I had *ever* been. If Jackson hadn't broken our kiss, I was quite certain I'd have demanded he take me right here in the kitchen.

"It's Squeaky," he murmured, his breath teasing along my ear and sending goose bumps chasing over my skin.

He held me close, and I loved it. I wanted to burrow into his strength and stay there forever. "Squeaky?" I asked his chest.

He laughed softly as he loosened his hold, and stepped away. "Yeah, Squeaky. See," he said, gesturing behind him.

I had met Squeaky earlier today when Jackson took me on the tour of the rescue area. "What's she doing in here?" I asked, as I turned to see the little pig standing in the doorway, a round white and black pig with her cute brown eyes blinking at us.

"Like I mentioned, she gets loose," he replied, as he knelt down and held his hand out. "When we first got her, Ash kept her in the house because she was little and she needed to be fed a lot. She's kind of spoiled."

Squeaky walked slowly and deliberately to Jackson, stopping and blinking up at him as Jackson knelt beside her. She looked over at me, so I leaned over and dragged my palm gently over her back. After another squeaking sound,

Jackson stood and walked to the refrigerator, pulling out a container with sliced apples. He handed her a slice, and she nibbled it up quickly.

Meanwhile, I stood in the kitchen, all kinds of hot and bothered, wondering what was more ridiculous. The fact that I came onto Jackson, and he kissed me senseless, or the fact that we'd been interrupted by a pig.

JACKSON

I leaned against the fence, watching as the horses trotted from the paddock by the barn toward the far corner in the pasture. Mischief had spent the night out there because that was usually his preference. He lifted his head, nickering softly as the rest of the horses approached him.

We were one of the few rescue programs that took horses in the area. Ash wanted to keep them all, but then she would keep every rescue that landed with us. I occasionally needed to point out that if we kept every animal we rescued, we would eventually be at capacity.

We tended to keep the ones she was most in love with, and those who fit in easily. Although Mischief could be considered a troublemaker, he was a good-natured gelding and got along well with all of the other horses. His mischievous nature related to his frustration with being penned up in a stall for any length of time. I surmised that came from his early days as a wild colt.

Mischief was a Banker horse, the breed of horse—or rather, pony, based on size—that lived wild on the Outer Banks of North Carolina. The wild horses were left to roam free on the islands as they had for centuries. They were descendants of Spanish horses, and small and hardy. They were largely left alone, with a few exceptions. Monitored by the National Park Service and a few private organizations, horses were occasionally culled due to illness.

Mischief had been culled from the herd, when both he and his mother were failing after she gave birth to the point there was concern both may not survive. Mischief was taken to a local vet and eventually made his way here when they were searching for a place for him to stay. We later learned his mother recovered on her own.

Meanwhile, Mischief, despite his small stature, was the boss of the herd here. He had a playful streak and was often teasing his fellow pasture mates. He was approaching four years old now. In his case, I was attached to him and had no plans to find another home for him. I intended to try to break him in soon. I idly wondered if Shay would want to ride him. She had been over here often when she was young, riding any horse her parents would let her climb on.

I thought Mischief would be a good fit for her. He was on the small side for me to ride, but he was just right for her. They had similar personalities, a bit guarded with an edge of feistiness.

I wondered at first if her feisty side had been snuffed out. After last night, I was quite certain that wasn't the case. I'd spent most of today trying to forget that crazy, hot kiss in the kitchen. I was still torn between disappointment that Squeaky interrupted us, and sheer relief.

I'd never forgotten our kiss years ago. There had been an indefinable, burning hot spark. But we'd been young, and I knew Remy would've strung me up if I made a play for his sister. It was enough of a mistake that I even let that first kiss happen.

So much had changed since then. It almost felt as if I were a different man when I kissed her this time. I was busy telling myself Shay was the reason why I couldn't let anything happen between us, but there was more to it.

She was my best friend's little sister. Sure, we were all adults now, but still. Tangled up inside that was what I knew she'd been through. Whatever happened for Shay next, she deserved a man who could give her everything. A man who could honor her and what she was—sunshine and steel, light and darkness, boldness and vulnerability.

I couldn't be the man she needed and deserved. I was quite certain it was best for me to stay a bachelor. I knew loss, far too well. It had been carved into my soul, etching bitterness and grief and leaving behind scars. I didn't need someone loving me and hoping for more, not when the darkness still claimed me at times.

With a mental shake, I pushed away from the fence and turned to head back to the barn. I was downstairs, literally counting bales of hay, when I heard footsteps coming down the hallway and Wade leaned in the doorway.

"Hey, boss, you think you have a few minutes to go over some scheduling stuff with me?" he asked.

Glancing up, I nodded. "Yeah, let me just finish this." I tapped in the last few numbers on my phone and turned to him. "Let's head to my office. I hate trying to look at the calendar on my phone for this stuff."

"Lead the way," Wade replied, following me down the barn aisle.

We headed up the stairs, turning into the hallway that led to the offices for the vet clinic. I nudged open the door to the office, my gaze catching sight of the papers scattered across the desk. I bit back a sigh. The administrative details associated with running the vet clinic, the lodge, and the rescue program were my least favorite part of the job.

Snagging my laptop, I slipped into a chair at the small round table in the corner. "Have a seat," I said, gesturing for Wade to sit across from me.

I had hired Wade the first summer I returned home.

Although I hadn't known him when I was younger, his family was from the area and lived on the outskirts of Asheville. After college, he'd traveled all over. He came with plenty of experience as a first responder, having mostly worked at a few outdoor resorts out West, running mountain climbing and hiking trips. He was totally dependable, easygoing, and a damn hard worker.

"Okay, let's take a look," I replied, as I pulled up our schedule and calendar. Aside from running the kitchen, Dani handled most of the scheduling through online bookings. She was a big fan of color-coding. At first, I thought it was silly. But I grew to love it. At a glance, I could look at the colors and know just how booked up we were.

Case in point, right now, I looked at the calendar and saw nothing but blue. Blue meant a date was booked with guests at the lodge, or any range of activities we coordinated for guests.

"Fuck."

Wade threw his head back with a laugh. "Exactly. We're booked. Starting next week, we got nothing open straight through summer, all the way to the end of October. I'm cool with that, but I guess we should decide if we want to add on some more guest cabins."

Pushing my laptop away on the table, I leaned back in my chair with a sigh. "I guess so. Problem is finding the time to make it happen."

"With Shay here helping with the rescue, does that free up any time for you?" Wade asked.

"Definitely some. But"—pausing, I gestured to the computer in front of us—"you're busy as hell. With that many dates booked, I know you'll be leading hikes galore. As it is, we talked about adding somebody to help with the overnight camping trips. Damn, this has gotten busy faster than I expected this year."

Wade cracked a smile, running a hand through his shaggy brown curls. "Told ya."

I rolled my eyes. "So you did." Leaning forward, I pulled the laptop back across the table, clicking out of that calendar into my personal calendar. This one showed my vet schedule.

Scanning it and clicking through the next few months, I could see the two days a week allocated for the clinic appointments were booked too. Since Ash was gone, gallivanting around following her rodeo boyfriend, I had picked up a few of her regulars. As a result, my schedule was getting tighter and tighter. I kept hoping Ash would stop wishing for more, but I knew better than to say anything. As it was, I had to bite my tongue too damn much when it came to her boyfriend. He'd never laid a hand on her, but I hated his laissez-faire attitude. She deserved better, but she reminded me again and again that they weren't serious. Whatever the fuck that meant.

"Well, I just won't add any more vet days," I commented. "I'm sure I can find time to work on those cabins here and there. I'll tell Dani to put up an ad, so we can recruit someone else to help with the hikes and whatnot. We need more help if we're booked solid."

"That'll work. I figure we can patchwork in between our crazy schedules to finish at least three or four of those cabins by the end of the summer. I'll do the grunt work with the guys, and you make it pretty," he said with a wink.

"Hey, I can do the grunt work too."

"Yeah, but I can't make high-end stuff like you."

After I got back from the war, I couldn't handle downtime. I needed something to do with my hands all the time. Aside from working myself to the bone, I started woodworking. What some people found tedious, I found soothing. It wasn't something I wanted to do more than occasionally, but I enjoyed putting the finishing touches on custom cabinetry and furniture. I didn't do it as much lately, in part because I was too damn busy, but also because I had found some shaky peace in the last year or so.

Wade's voice broke into my thoughts. "Aside from helping with the rescue, anything else Shay can help with?"

"That'll keep her busy, but I'm gonna ask Dani to chat with her about handling some office stuff and the online end of things. Shay's pretty good with computers."

Wade nodded. "Just a heads-up, that new temp we hired to help clear the new pasture has got his sights set on her."

I had no idea why the hell Wade thought I'd give a damn. I knew he'd likely seen Shay's name splashed in the news when her ex got arrested for assaulting her. We hadn't spoken of it, but for anyone who paid even a little bit of attention to the local news, it was impossible to avoid. Her ex's father was a long-time politician in North Carolina. Clint Glover Sr. had every expectation his son would follow in his footsteps. Then, he nearly beat Shay to death in the parking lot of the condominium complex where they lived in Chapel Hill.

The news had speculated for weeks on just what she'd done wrong to trigger the whole mess. Then, Clint Jr. slammed into a car while he was drunk, killing two people. That news eclipsed the story about him and Shay. Thank fucking God.

For some reason, hearing that anyone even noticed Shay that way set me on edge. A bolt of possessiveness hit me. I had no right to lay any claim on Shay, but I sure as hell wasn't going to sit around and watch somebody else sniff around her feet.

I held Wade's gaze and arched a brow. "Seriously?"

Wade rolled his eyes. "Hell yeah. He's just a kid fresh out of college, young and horny. And she's beautiful. Also, none of my damn business, but if you were hoping it wasn't obvious that you had a thing for her, it's *really* obvious," he said bluntly.

One of the things I loved about Wade was he didn't tiptoe around anything. However, at the moment, I found that tendency slightly annoying.

I shook my head. "Shay *is* beautiful, but that doesn't mean I have a thing for her. Whatever the hell that is. And you're right, it's none your damn business."

Wade chuckled. "Nice to see somebody get to you."

"Hey, why don't you worry about your own love life?" I countered.

"I don't have one, dude."

"You and Dani."

Wade went quiet for a few beats, his lips thinning and his eyes narrowing. "There is nothing going on between me and Dani."

"You just keep bullshitting. Maybe you'll convince yourself sooner than the rest of us."

Wade chuckled, shaking his head. "Sure. Word of advice, though," he said as he turned.

"What's that?"

"Maybe not the best move to have Shay shacked up in the house with you. Unless you plan to do something about her."

At that, he left my office, closing the door behind him. Roughly a minute passed when I realized the last thing I needed to do was sit in my office and try to focus on the work I had the most trouble paying any attention to. Ash and I had been discussing hiring an actual office manager, and I toyed again with the idea of talking with Shay about it.

What should've been an easy conversation had trepidation running through me. Shay affected me too easily. For the most part, or so I liked to tell myself, I had battened down the hatches inside. After my time in Iraq, I knew I would never lose the sense of pride I carried with me. My father and my grandfather had both served in the Marines. I had followed in their footsteps, straight into a Special Operations team. Yet, one mission had left me with scars on my body, my heart, and my mind.

Teasing out the sensibilities of something like a relationship was out of the question. I had nightmares occasionally and still struggled with a sense of deep grief. I knew I was shut down emotionally and that was perfectly fine with me. I was at loose ends after I returned from the war. I would've traded my dad being alive, but inheriting the farm had given me something to focus on, a sense of purpose.

I could hold the painful memories at bay and still feel like I had something to give to the world. Taking care of animals and being outside for most of my days in some capacity helped keep me sane. I was no monk. Yet, I took care of those needs with as least fuss as possible. Casual hookups were the most I could handle. It was an exchange of mutual benefit—quick, clean, and with no complications.

Shay was one giant walking complication—a beautiful, sexy-as-hell complication who had somehow reached inside me and set hooks in my heart.

I hadn't actually spent the night—sleeping, that is—with a woman in years. My last dating relationship had been before I went overseas. Even then, I couldn't say romance had been a priority. These days, my priority was keeping my sanity and not having anyone expect too much from me. It was enough to have my sister and the hodgepodge of friends and staff rely on me.

I couldn't consider managing the expectations of a relationship. The simple concept of sleeping in the same bed as someone had tension knotting in my gut. I hated it when the nightmares hit. I didn't need someone feeling bad for me about that.

Abruptly, I glanced at the clock and realized I'd been dwelling on this for a solid ten minutes and hadn't gotten a damn thing done. If Shay was going to be here, she was a distraction on her own. I might as well see if she wanted to help with this part of the business. I didn't quite know how long she planned to stay. All I knew was Remy was concerned and didn't want her living on her own. I doubted she knew how worried he was. He asked me to ask Ash to call her about coming here.

Of course, Ash had been happy to do that. As Shay's good friend, she was worried about her too. I didn't know if any of us knew much more about what happened than what had been splashed in the news. I had enough sense to know there was likely far more to the story. There always was.

With a swift mental kick, I ordered myself to stop dwelling on Shay. I slammed out of my office, thinking maybe today was a good day to try putting a saddle blanket on Mischief.

Chapter Nine

SHAY

"Hey, sis, how you doing?" Remy said after I answered his call.

I idly traced my fingertip along the edge of the sink as I looked out the window. The sun was bright, casting one side of the valley in shadow in the distance.

"I'm good."

"You all settled in?" he asked, his familiar drawl a comfort, yet I could hear the unspoken worry in his tone.

I adored my brother. Always had. Even when we were little and he teased me occasionally, he'd been a patient older brother, one I could always count on. Much as I felt blessed to have him, regret and guilt stung sharply when I thought of how thoroughly I'd screwed up my life.

"Of course I am. It's not like I'm living alone, Remy. I just got to the farm yesterday. Ash is out of town for the month, but Jackson's here. You know he won't let a hair on my head get hurt."

"I know."

Though Remy rarely mentioned how much he worried about me, I could always sense it. Or, I thought I could.

Perhaps it was my own need to push back against that worry. To show the world I didn't need anyone to worry about me.

"I don't know why you're so concerned. I've got Jackson to boss me around just as much as you do. You don't need to worry about me anymore, Remy. I swear."

After our parents died, I hated how alone I felt because I hadn't had the courage to tell Remy what was happening until it was too late.

"And you don't need to tell me not to worry," he countered with a teasing tone.

It was just enough to nudge me out of spinning into an internal quagmire. I laughed, the tension easing slightly inside. "Fine then. Tell me how you're doing. Is it spring there yet?"

"Well, since we talked just yesterday morning, there's a little bit less snow on the ground today and it's getting muddier," he replied, referencing our call while I'd been driving. Bless his heart, but he'd answered the phone even though I'd called him well before dawn because I wasn't thinking about the four-hour time difference from here to Alaska.

"Right, but you said things melt fast there once they start."

"That I did, sis."

"Hang on a sec," I said, turning when I heard the front door to the farmhouse open.

Jackson's voice echoed down the hall. "Just stopped by to grab a lead."

"Okay," I called mostly to no one because the door opened and shut as I spoke. Jackson wasn't one to slow down and wait. I presumed he'd snagged the long horse lead I'd noticed hanging on the hooks in the hallway.

"Sorry about that," I said, turning my attention back to Remy on the phone.

"No problem. I gotta go. There's a car on the side of the road. I'm gonna check and make sure they're okay."

"Of course you are. You take care of everybody, Remy. I love you."

"Love you too, sis. I'll talk to you soon."

I smiled as I slipped my phone into my pocket. Hearing Remy's voice almost always lifted my spirits.

I busied myself putting away the dishes and tidying the kitchen. When I turned back to the window a few minutes later, Jackson was in the small paddock with Mischief. He had Mischief on a lunging line, although he wasn't trying to lunge him. He was letting him meander around the paddock.

Mischief's coat was brushed to a gloss and glinted under the sun. He kept turning his head and trying to bite at the saddle pad Jackson had carefully placed on his back. If I was being honest with myself, I was more mesmerized by watching Jackson than Mischief. With his jeans sitting low on his hips and his T-shirt discarded, his bronzed skin gleamed in the sun. Of course he was a sight to behold. I could look at him for days and never tire of the view.

Yet, his obscenely fit body wasn't what had me so enraptured. No, it was his patience and gentleness with the half-wild horse. It had been probably ten years since I'd ridden a horse. After I finished high school, I simply hadn't had the time, nor the funds.

If I hadn't been friends with Ash growing up, it's doubtful I'd have ever had a chance to ride as much as I did. I was curious to know if Jackson intended to train Mischief for English or Western-style riding. I knew from Ash that Jackson did both. I personally preferred English-style riding because that meant jumping, which I loved. Recalling Mischief's easy jump over the four-foot high fence surrounding the pasture, I didn't doubt he would take to that easily.

I'd spent the last twenty minutes or so watching Jackson groom Mischief and then carefully lay the saddle pad on Mischief's back. He finally cinched it on with a lightweight cotton girth. After that point, Mischief wasn't too thrilled that he couldn't shake off the saddle pad. I laughed when he nipped at it again before turning to look at Jackson.

If it weren't for that crazy kiss last night, I would be out there right now, asking Jackson questions. But, I wasn't quite sure what to do right now. A funny thing had happened though. Seeing as I'd sworn off men, I expected myself to back down after my temporary insanity last night. But I didn't want to. Not at all.

Jackson would be the perfect man to get me over my irrational fear of sex. I wasn't afraid of sex, not exactly. I was just unsettled, restless and far too worried about it. The chemistry burning between Jackson and me was hot enough I thought perhaps it might override my anxiety.

With Jackson, I wasn't worried about him suddenly getting rough. He was a good man, down to the bone. After the details I gleaned from Dani, I figured I could assume he didn't want a relationship any more than I did. That made it even more perfect. It didn't need to be complicated with expectations.

Somehow, Jackson made me forget the layers and layers of insecurity that had piled on in the aftermath of what happened with Clint.

After a few more minutes of watching, I turned and headed outside. I might as well just do what I wanted. I didn't need to surreptitiously watch. Sure, I wanted to be closer to Jackson and might just have to hold myself back from staring at his glorious chest, but I was curious and wanted to see what his plans were for Mischief. I liked that little horse. He'd already burrowed into my heart, and I hoped like hell Jackson didn't intend to try to find someone else to take him.

Striding out of the farmhouse, I approached the paddock situated between the barn and pasture. "Hey there," I called as I leaned against the railing.

Jackson turned and lifted his hand in a wave. Meanwhile, Mischief came trotting over, yanking the lunging lead out of

Jackson's hands. I laughed when Mischief reached me. Glancing past him, I caught Jackson's eye as he approached. "Sorry, I didn't mean to distract him."

Jackson grinned and shrugged. "A bird flying through the sky distracts him."

I reached out to scratch behind Mischief's ears. Jackson stopped by the fence. When I looked over at him, I instantly came to the conclusion he should *not* be allowed to walk around without his shirt on.

"Really?" Jackson countered, a devilish glint entering his eyes.

Apparently, I actually said that thought out loud. Fuck my life. It was too late to try to repair that blunder. I shrugged, as nonchalantly as possible. "I can't be the first person who's mentioned that."

"Uh, you are," Jackson replied, a slow grin stretching across his face.

My cheeks were on fire. "Oh well. I hope you don't see your vet appointments like that, at least."

He threw his head back with a laugh. "No. I keep my shirt on for vet appointments. I don't know why you're worried about that, though. It's not like my animal patients care about what I'm wearing."

"Oh, it's not the animals I'm worried about. Anyway," I said brightly, deciding an abrupt change in subject was in order," I was curious how it's going with Mischief."

With me idly stroking his neck, Mischief had finally stopped trying to bite at the saddle pad.

Jackson slid his hand over Mischief's rump before checking the tension on the girth. "I'm gonna take this off now because he's not actually biting at it. It went about as well as expected with him. He's an easygoing guy, but super curious. Certainly not the worst horse I've tried to train."

"Can I help?" My question flew out. As soon as it did, I wanted to take it back. Because I wanted this. Perhaps a bit too much.

Jackson answered easily. "Of course. Might as well. He likes you anyway. Ever broken a half-wild horse?"

I shook my head. "I haven't ridden since I used to ride here with Ash. I rode a few green ponies, but that's about it. Tell me what to do, and I'll do it."

Jackson was simply looking at me. The moment my words came out, his eyes darkened. "Well, right now, I just want him to put up with the saddle pad for about fifteen minutes every day. He's so green, all he's used to is a halter and a lead. We'll take it nice and slow."

With the saddle pad in hand, he reached up and unbuckled Mischief's halter. "Mind hanging onto this for a minute?" he asked, holding up the halter and saddle pad.

I reached across the fence. "Of course not." My fingers brushed Jackson's as I curled my hand around the halter, a hot zing of electricity racing up my arm.

"Come on, buddy," he said to Mischief, running his hand over his back. "Let's get you out with your friends for the afternoon."

Mischief followed him over to the gate that led out to the full pasture. Just like yesterday when I arrived, as soon as Jackson opened the gate, Mischief lifted his head and took off at a quick trot, aiming straight for the horses gathered in the corner of the pasture in a shady area near a small pond.

Jackson stepped out of the paddock, checking to make sure the gate was latched before walking to my side and fetching the halter and saddle pad from me. The moment he was close, my pulse did a little dance. I remembered the feel of his hard body against mine, the mere thought of it sending a rush of heat through me and my sex clenching in response.

"Come on, I'll show you where we keep the tack and whatnot."

I followed him into the cool, quiet of the barn. In here, they had the horses downstairs, with offices for the vet clinic upstairs. This barn hadn't been here before. It was built into a slope with the parking lot to the vet clinic level with the upper floor. The downstairs had two rows of stalls with a wide aisle in between, and storage rooms along another hallway, that portion of the structure built into the slope.

I loved the smell of a barn—the scent of hay, a hint of leather lingering in the air, and the earthy scents of horses and grain. A little bird flew by, chirping as it landed in a small nest on a shelf above one of the stalls.

Jackson's eyes flicked up with a wry grin. "The birds do as they please, and I leave them be. Ash gave me a lecture one year when I tried to deal with a few too many nests. They shit everywhere, but otherwise, it's no bother."

Leading me into the hallway at the back, he pushed open a door. We stepped into a room with shelving and bins along one wall, and tack hanging on the other with saddle racks and hooks for bridles and more. It was quite organized.

Jackson hung the halter on a hook by the door and tossed the saddle pad onto a stack of them on a shelf. "This is where you'll find all kinds of odds and ends, including the feed. We don't ride a whole lot around here anymore. We have a few horses we use for trail rides for the guests, but the rest are rescues, so it's a crapshoot whether they're even trained. Wish I had more time to ride, but it's hit or miss unless I have a project like Mischief. Think you can handle doing what I did today on your own?"

"You mean trying the saddle pad with him?"

"That's it."

"In that case, yes," I replied.

We were standing beside the door, which had shut behind us on a spring hinge. I became acutely aware of just how close we happened to be standing. There was perhaps a foot separating us. The moment my awareness struck, a riff of sensation traveled over my skin, my body tightening in anticipation.

"I meant to ask you about something else," Jackson said.

"What's that?"

"How do you feel about office work?"

"Feel?"

"We could use some help with the office stuff. It falls to the wayside, especially when Ash isn't here. I'd be more than grateful for anything you can do to help," he explained with a sheepish smile.

I suddenly felt insecure, uncertain if there had been a conversation about money and me staying here. "Look, I don't have any rent money right now, but give me a couple months, and I'm sure I can scrounge something up for work."

Jackson stared at me blankly. "Huh?"

"I'm happy to do office work and anything else you need. I'll work for free," I added hurriedly.

Jackson still had that blank look on his face. Cocking his head to the side, he replied, "I'm not asking you to work for free. Any work you do here, you'll be paid for."

"I will?"

"Shay, almost everybody who works here lives here. You don't think I don't pay anybody, do you?"

Embarrassment washed through me, my cheeks getting hot. Shifting on my feet, I chewed on the inside of my cheek. "I didn't know. Look, I don't know how much Remy told you—or Ash, for that matter—but I really need this. I don't want it to seem like I'm taking advantage and just assuming I could stay here without pulling my weight. I didn't know if I needed to pay rent."

Jackson was quiet for a few beats before he nodded slowly. "Fair enough. Well, I expected we would be paying you for any work you did. For almost everyone else who works here, lodging is part of the deal. So, it's the same for you. I guess I assumed Ash explained this to you."

"Really?" Although I was still swimming in mortification —for being in the mess I was in, for needing help this much, for carrying the weight of shame and worthlessness Clint had saddled me with—I was almost giddy with relief.

Jackson chuckled softly. "Look, when Ash and I decided to try to do this after Dad passed away, we wanted to do it right. So, we pay people well and staff get lodging if they need it. The lodge more than covers the costs. The rescue doesn't make any money, but it pays for itself. We have donations to help with that. Any office work you can help with would be amazing. Trust me, I'm not offering it up just to give you something to do. I'm asking because I'm too damn busy, and I hate it. Ash helps out when she's around, but lately, she hasn't been around too much."

I sensed Jackson probably had an opinion about that, but I figured now wasn't the time to bring it up. "Well, I'm happy to help. I actually like office stuff. Whatever you need, I'll take care of it. I hate being bored."

Jackson's lips kicked up into a smile. "I know that feeling."

As he stood there, looking at me, an electric heat washed over me. My skin was tingling, my belly alive with butterflies. It was quiet in the small room, and I became keenly aware of the energy suspended in the air. Jackson's presence was strong. He was hardened, roughened around the edges, exuding a quiet intensity.

"Shay..." he began. His voice fell into the quiet.

I didn't wait to hear what he had to say next.

Chapter Ten

SHAY

The old me, the brave, teasing me, made her presence known. I wanted to nudge Jackson, to remind him just how hot our kiss had been last night. All it took was one step, and I was right there. "Kiss me," I said.

Jackson's nostrils flared, and his eyes widened slightly before narrowing. "I'm not so sure that's a good idea."

"I think it's a great idea," I countered, a corner of my mind watching in amazement. I reached out, placing my palm on his chest. I knew I hadn't been imagining he was aroused. My hips bumped his, and I felt his hard arousal. A part of me startled, but I ignored it, focusing instead on the heat blooming from my core.

Something flashed in his eyes. "Fuck," he muttered.

Just like last night, the collision of our lips was fierce, and then Jackson instantly gentled, drawing back slightly, brushing his lips back and forth across mine.

Dear God. This man was going to slay me. Our kiss dissolved into a heated, sensual tease. With seductive nips, darts of his tongue inside my mouth, each one teasing me just a little bit more, I molded myself to him, melting like lava inside.

Jackson had this opposing effect on me. My need for him was so great, I was restless and anxious, bordering on frantic for more. At the same time, I felt caught in a web of languid desire. I could kiss him forever.

He took his time, drawing back to dust kisses at the corners of my mouth, sliding across my lips, and then sweeping his tongue inside when I gasped. He took a step, nudging me until my back bumped the door. One palm curved over my bottom, holding me tight against his arousal. The other cupped my nape, his thumb brushing over the wild beat of my pulse along the side of my neck.

When he lifted his head, I was gasping, gulping in air, my heart thudding so hard and fast, my entire body was vibrating from the beat. Jackson dusted kisses along my jawline before he caught the sensitive lobe of my ear in his teeth and sent hot shivers racing through me.

I was hyper-aware of the hard length of his arousal, cradled at the apex of my thighs. His calloused palm scattered sparks over the surface of my skin when his touch slid up under my T-shirt. His lips traveled down my neck, each point of contact sending slivers of fire through me, every sensation spinning to my core.

Somewhere along the way, his knee slipped between my thighs, creating just enough pressure that my hips were rocking over it, sweet, piercing jolts of pleasure making me gasp. My sex clenched. Jackson made me wet by simply getting close. Throw in a kiss for the ages, and I was drenched with arousal. The moment he put his hands on me, I melted like butter.

"Jesus, Shay," Jackson muttered, his rough drawl making me tight inside.

Dear God, this man might be able to make me come just from talking. He flicked the clasp between my breasts, roughly shoving my shirt up. "Fuck, even better than I remembered."

His mouth closed over a nipple, the warm, slick suction making me cry out as I buried a hand in his hair and held on. I was wearing jeans, not exactly conducive for anything quick and easy, but I was finding not much got in Jackson's way. While he was teasing my nipples, alternating between them with licks, light pinches, and his teeth grazing over them, he had my zipper down in no time and lifted my knee, making room to tease his fingers into my panties.

He murmured against my breast, the vibration alone making my pussy clench. "So wet, so sweet."

His fingers slid across my clit, swollen and wet. He sank one finger, and then another, inside of me, the tight space limiting motion, creating intense pressure while his thumb circled over my clit.

Lifting his head, he murmured, "I need to taste that sweetness."

Dragging my eyes open, I watched as he drew his fingers out, placed one, and then the other, in his mouth as he tasted my juices.

It was the hottest thing I'd ever seen. I'd never had a man talk to me the way he did—endearments mingled with the slightest bit of dirty talk.

"Delicious," he murmured, that single word making my pussy clench.

I almost came, a piercing throb of pleasure weakening my knees. Then, his lips were on mine again, and I tasted the salty evidence of my arousal in his kiss as he buried his fingers inside my pussy again.

My climax was swift and devastating. His thumb pressed down on my clit. With two thick fingers buried inside me, the pressure that had built inside spun loose so abruptly I cried out. My head banged against the door behind me, and my body shuddered roughly, my channel clamping down around his fingers.

Jackson caught my cry in our kiss, teasing me a bit more with his fingers as the shudders slowed. He gradually gentled our kiss, his lips brushing across mine as he slowly drew his hand out. The sound of him pulling up my zipper was loud in the quiet space.

"We've got company."

I was so stunned, so disoriented, I didn't even hear the sound of footsteps until Jackson said something.

He moved quickly, stepping back. In a matter of seconds, he tugged my clothes into place. All the while, I simply leaned against the door, barely able to pull myself together, with pings of pleasure echoing through my body.

Voices passed by the door. "Yeah, I thought he came in here, but I guess not," Dani said.

"I'll go check his office," Wade replied.

"Shay," Jackson said, his tone low.

I gave my head a little shake and pushed away from the door. I wanted to say something, but clearly, now was not the time.

"You stay here, I'm gonna head out there. Wait a few minutes, and the coast should be clear."

"Where should I go?" I asked, so disoriented I didn't even know where the hell to go.

"Well, since Dani's here, it would be the perfect time to come upstairs. We'll check in about the office stuff."

I felt myself nodding. Jackson stood before me, something flickering in his gaze, but I didn't know how to read it. After a moment, he nodded and turned away.

Chapter Eleven

JACKSON

"It's perfect!" Dani exclaimed, clapping her hands. "Even when Ash is here, all of us are too busy. This could just be Shay's job. That, and the rescue stuff."

"Works for me. As it is, we're way behind on accounting, and our website is out of date. If you can keep up with the reservations for the lodge, I'll let her take over the rest. Once she's up to speed, I think you can hand that over too," I suggested.

"Sounds like a plan to me," Dani replied. She paused, her eyes narrowing as she regarded me. "I like Shay."

"Shay's great," I said, as I surveyed the wreckage of my desk with papers scattered across it.

"Of course she's great. But I mean, I *really* like her. I think you like her too."

I looked across my desk at Dani. "Of course I like her. She's like family. I mean, her brother's one of my best friends, and she and Ash used to be really close," I said, fighting not to think about what had just happened in the tack room. Losing control wasn't a problem for me.

Shay sent me skidding sideways inside. She ripped my control right out of my hands and made me half-crazy.

Dani cocked her head to the side. "You're dancing around what I mean and you know it, which proves me right. You have a thing for Shay. I think she'd be good for you," she said, pursing her lips and pinning me with her bossy look.

I ran a hand through my hair. "Oh, for fuck's sake, Dani. Don't get started on your matchmaking. You tried to set me up with that girl who worked here last summer. Shay's an old friend. Don't try to do that with her."

"*That* girl has a name, it's Tiffany," she said sharply.

I sighed. "Right, Tiffany. I didn't mean to be rude. You make it sound like I forgot the name of someone I used to date. *Nothing* happened, so don't make it something it wasn't. That was your agenda, not mine. Can we drop this please?"

Conveniently, there was a knock at the door. In the few minutes since I left Shay behind in the tack room, I still had the taste of her arousal on my tongue, Wade had come and gone, and Dani remained behind when I told her I wanted to talk about my idea to have Shay pick up the slack with the administrative side of things.

"Come in," I called, expecting to see Shay and bracing myself for my body's reaction.

She stepped through the door, glancing from me to Dani. "Should I close the door?" she asked.

I had only closed it behind Wade when he left solely because I needed some kind of warning when she showed up. "No need."

"Okay." Her expression was controlled, but her cheeks were still a little flushed and her lips were swollen from our kisses. I ordered myself not to think about the way her pussy felt clenching around my fingers when she flew apart. She slipped into the chair beside Dani, across from my desk.

I dove right into talking, anything to keep me from thinking too hard. "I was just telling Dani that we discussed having you take over the office stuff, and she's all on board. I figured we could go over everything now, while we're all here. I'm gonna be honest, things are a bit of a mess. Dani handles the scheduling for the lodge, but Ash and I handle the vet clinic scheduling, and the supply orders for the farm and the lodge, except for the kitchen. Ash usually takes care of the website for the rescue, and fields calls for requests to take new animals and coordinate potential adoptions. I fly by the seat of my pants, and Ash has only been here every other month or so."

Dani chuckled. "Both of you fly by the seat of your pants when it comes to this stuff. It's kind of a miracle this place is running okay. We could really use someone who could just make this their job."

Shay looked between us. "I'm happy to help. Why don't you show me where to start? If it's disorganized, I'll get it organized."

The three of us settled at the round table in my office. I didn't know whether Dani did it on purpose or not, but she moved over when I came to sit down, which meant I had no choice but to sit in the chair between them. I could smell the scent of Shay, which left me distracted as hell.

I breathed a sigh of relief when it was all over. Dani appeared to sense I was getting irritable and took Shay with her over to the lodge, ostensibly to show her the online calendar she used for scheduling.

As soon as they left, I pulled up the trip calendar and saw one was scheduled for tonight. The best thing would be for me to get the hell out of here.

———

I lay on my sleeping bag in the darkness, looking up at the night sky. Although spring was here, it was still cool when you were close to five thousand feet above sea level. There was a bite to the air, crisp and invigorating. The stars were strewn above like diamonds on velvet.

I wished I could blame the cool air for my lack of sleep. Among many reasons for taking on my father's dream, I found peace when I was outside. I also found animals far less complicated than humans.

Usually a few days of hiking and sleeping outside was refreshing, a true break from the busyness of my day-to-day work around the lodge. Yet tonight, I was restless in large part because I had taken this guided trip out of Wade's hands mainly to try and escape Shay. Or rather, my undeniable attraction to her and how quickly it was spiraling out of my control.

I was wide awake after a five-mile hike, when I should've been fucking tired, because I couldn't stop thinking about Shay. I'd replayed our encounter in the tack room a few too many times already. Just thinking about it now, and electric heat spun through me. She was fucking glorious when she let go.

She was also dangerous. As soon as she asked me to kiss her, I lost my damn mind. I knew, I fucking knew, the first kiss was bad enough. But what happened today? Damn. When I buried my fingers in her sweet pussy, I was done for.

She ruined me, slayed me. I wasn't even a guy who talked much when it came to sex. With her, I couldn't fucking shut up. The taste of her hit me like a drug. I almost groaned aloud as I lay in the darkness on a sleeping bag two-thirds of the way up a mountain. The group I was guiding was conveniently four different couples. They were mere feet away from me in tents, and here I was, ready to go another round with a woman who wasn't even with me.

As I drifted in and out of a restless sleep that night, I told myself I just needed a few days to get myself together. I'd be able to handle it.

"So, will the following Wednesday work for your appointment?" I asked politely.

"Well, I guess it'll have to do," the woman said, a curt edge to her tone.

"Dr. Stone will certainly appreciate your understanding. I have Brandy down for next Wednesday, okay? Thank you so much."

This was my tenth phone call. Jackson had decided, without any notice whatsoever, to pick up one of the hiking trips and lead a group up a nearby mountain to spend two nights. The return day landed on one of his vet clinic days. With only two days scheduled each week for the clinic, it didn't leave much room for moving appointments around.

My transition into managing the office end of things, so to speak, had been a skid. I'd spent more time than I preferred apologizing for the abrupt rescheduling of people's beloved pet appointments.

I wanted to tell them I was probably more frustrated than they were. Because, you see, Jackson hadn't even bothered to tell me he was leaving either. I discovered that little tidbit when I returned to the house to change and Dani called over to invite me down for dinner in the lodge. When I arrived, everyone seemed to think I would know why Jackson had decided to lead the trip.

I had no clue. Although, I sensed it had something to do with our wildly-out-of-control encounter in the tack room.

I was pissed. I didn't have any expectations, but a little courtesy would have been nice.

With a sigh, I glanced at the computer calendar in front of me, relieved to see I had successfully rescheduled all of the appointments. Standing from the desk, I stretched and looked around the office. It was rather bare bones. There was a picture of Ash and Jackson together when they were kids, alongside a photo of Jackson and Remy during one of their visits here.

I remembered that halcyon summer—a hot, hazy summer in the mountains. Long days riding horses with Ash, lazy days spent by any number of mountains, lakes, and rivers, where we could cool off in the water. My parents were still alive, and the world felt as if it held me in a summer cocoon.

It was the summer after I graduated from high school and before I started college. I was young and, upon reflection, startlingly innocent. I had no idea I would start dating a man a few years later who would rob me of trust and all sense of safety. Beyond the terror of experiencing Clint's abuse, it was the lingering aftereffects that had their claws in me.

That summer was a few years before Jackson and Remy stayed with me for a weekend and that silly kiss happened. Before I met Clint and my world skidded off its tracks in private, while everything looked perfectly fine on the outside.

Jackson hadn't quite rocked my world with our first kiss, but he had now. Twice. Even though it had been two days since he left, every time I replayed it—which was quite a bit

—my body still reverberated from the climax he had given me with his fingers.

Just thinking about it now, my skin got hot. Every time I recalled the look on his face when he licked my arousal off his fingers, I nearly melted on the spot.

I spun around quickly, my eyes landing on the messy desk just as I heard footsteps coming up the stairs. With the hardwood floors and stairs, it was impossible for anyone to sneak up on me here. Not many staff ventured over here. There were a few guys who helped out with the horses and the rescues, but people rarely came up to the offices. The lodge was definitely busier, and it was much closer to the staff lodging. It hadn't escaped my attention I was the only person other than Jackson staying at the farmhouse. I knew if Ash were here, she'd be staying there as well. But for now, she wasn't here.

I wasn't sure how to interpret that, or if there was anything to even interpret.

Dani stopped in the doorway, flashing a bright smile. Her brown curls were pulled up in her usual ponytail, her green eyes crinkling at the corners. She tended to wear jeans and cowboy boots paired with a T-shirt, and today was no exception. In the kitchen, she stuck to comfortable tennis shoes.

"Hey, thought I'd come over and see how things were going. I was just thinking maybe it's convenient Jackson's gone for a few days. You can totally take over the office. Let's organize this place," she said, strolling in and sitting down in the chair at the round table in the corner.

"Coffee?" I asked as I stepped over to the small table by the wall where a fresh pot of coffee was waiting. "I just made some a little while ago. It's nice and dark."

"I'd love a cup," she replied.

I quickly filled two mugs, holding them in one hand as I grabbed a couple of creamers and sugars in the other. Sitting down at the table across from her, I slid a cup over to her. "Didn't know if you liked cream or sugar, so I brought both."

"I like it black, or with just a dash of cream."

"I'll split a creamer with you," I replied as I opened one. At her nod, I poured half in my mug and handed it over. After I took a few sips, I leaned back in my chair with a sigh. "Do you think it's okay for me to organize the office however I want?"

Dani shrugged. "Of course." She waved her hand toward the messy desk. "Jackson isn't very organized here, which tells you how much he hates it. I mean, hell, he's a Marine. His schedule is set in fucking stone. He knows he's got to deal with the admin stuff for this place to run, but he's never really developed a system. Ash has done a little better, but she's here and there. Ever since she met Kyle, she hasn't been here as much."

I wanted to be nosy about Ash, but I didn't feel quite right about prying. She was one of my closest friends and had been there for me even after we grew apart, when Clint isolated me from all of my friends.

Dani cocked her head to the side. "Don't be afraid to ask questions. I'm sure you've heard enough comments about Ash's boyfriend to realize we all think he's kind of a jerk," she said, effectively demonstrating her mind-reading abilities.

I took a deep breath and let it out with a sigh. "I gathered. Please tell me he's not hurting her."

"Oh, hell no. God, I think he's an ass, but I'm not gonna pin that on him. No. It's just that he's a player. He's handsome as the devil too. He wooed her, and she fell for it. She claims that she's not looking for anything serious, but while he's busy fucking around, she's not with anybody other than him. She acts like it's not a big deal that they're just friends with benefits, but that's not her personality," Dani explained.

I nodded and took a sip of coffee. "Definitely not. I know it tore her up when things fell apart with Brian." Ash got engaged right around the time I met Clint. There were lots of holes in what I knew about what happened for her and most of my friends while I was with Clint. Mostly because I hardly talked to anyone. In spite of that, Ash had been there for me one hundred percent when I called her for help.

All I knew was her fiancé had been screwing around on her, and she found out when one of his side girlfriends sent her photographs of them via text. Yay for modern modes of communication.

Dani continued, not seeming to notice or care I didn't have much to offer. "I guess, the way I look at it, she was at a low point, and he swooped in. I hope she moves on sooner rather than later. Jackson's been more than overwhelmed since Ash hasn't been around to help as much. It's a godsend that you're here."

"I'm glad. I didn't want to be a burden coming here. When Ash talked to me about this, the timing was perfect."

Dani sipped her coffee. Although I had briefly glossed over what happened with Clint, I didn't want to keep it hidden. "As you probably know from the news, Clint beat me badly one night. I'm okay, but it was a mess to get out of it. Ash and Jackson are good friends, and it was just what I needed when they offered to let me come here. I'm relieved to actually be able to do something here."

My words came out in a rush. I had meant to say them matter-of-factly because I'd been practicing that. Instead, my throat clogged with emotion, and I wanted to cry.

Dani's warm eyes softened, and she reached over, catching my hand in hers and giving it a squeeze. "We're all glad you're here. You don't have to explain anything about what happened or why you're here."

"I know," I said, swiping away the single tear that escaped. "I just don't like pretending like nothing happened. That's what I did for years. Everything just got crazy. After I started dating Clint, my parents died and that was really hard. By the time things got really ugly with Clint, I had nowhere to go.

"My brother, who I'm really close to, Jackson's friend"—I paused, pointing to the photograph on the wall—"didn't know what was going on because I was so embarrassed. I lost everything, so I really needed a place to land. It's amazing that y'all are so welcoming. I feel a little weird being at the house. I mean, I know Jackson and he's Remy's best friend, but I'm closer to Ash. Do you think maybe I should ask him about moving to one of the cabins?" I asked.

Dani smiled softly and paused to sip her coffee, her gaze considering. "Well, that was suggested, but Ash made the call that she wanted you to be at the house. I don't know how Jackson would feel about you moving out. Want me to ask him?"

"No, no. I can ask him. I just don't want to impose."

"Trust me, you're not imposing. Doesn't matter how you ended up here, you're welcome and we legitimately need your help. Sometimes fate throws things in our path. I think this is exactly where you're supposed to be."

My throat tightened with emotion again. On the heels of a deep breath, I managed a small smile. "I hope so. Back to lighter topics, do you really think I could just reorganize this office? I don't want to rearrange furniture or anything, but the desk is a train wreck."

"Tackle the desk, and do whatever you'd like to organize the vet clinic scheduling and manage the ordering. I handle the scheduling for the lodge. When you're up to speed, I'll hand it over. I've got enough on my plate as it is. Ash and Jackson usually deal with all the rescue stuff, managing the nonprofit side, and dealing with ordering, accounts, and reports. They also keep the website up-to-date, posting things when we're looking for homes for rescues, fundraising for the rescue, and so on. For the clinic, that's mostly scheduling. I do all the ordering for the kitchen, but they handle the rest, and then there's payroll."

I stared at Dani, my mouth slowly dropping open. "You

mean to tell me Jackson and Ash handle all that, on top of everything else? That's like a job and a half."

Dani nodded slowly. "Exactly. That's why we need you. In fact, you better be prepared because you're not gonna be able to leave."

Chapter Thirteen

JACKSON

The trip ended up being a long three days. My plan turned out to be a spectacular failure. Instead of succeeding at loosening Shay's hold in my thoughts, the opposite occurred.

One of the things I loved about being in the outdoors was the way I could clear my mind. Most of the time, I appreciated the lack of distraction. In this case, it was a source of great frustration. The couples on this trip wanted to summit a peak—at sunrise, specifically. Rising in the moonlit early morning was no trouble, considering my sleep was restless every single night, with Shay sashaying through my thoughts, teasing me, and keeping me awake.

With the silvery moon lighting our way, we made our way to the summit just in time for sunrise. The sky was cloudy, which created a gorgeous array of colors, although I knew rain was threatening. I could feel it in the air and see it in the clouds. The group got some amazing photographs, and we headed back down the mountain.

On the way down, a steady drizzle began to fall, and the ground was slick in a few spots. One of the women slipped on a rock. When I reached out to catch her, I overextended my arm, leaving my shoulder sore and throbbing for the rest of the hike down the mountain.

I figured a few days of rest was all I needed. Late that afternoon, Wade met us at the arranged upon pickup spot at the trailhead. "Hey, man," he called, as he stepped out of the van we used to ferry guests from the lodge to various points for our trips.

"Hey, how were things at the lodge this weekend?" I replied.

"Quite all right." His eyes narrowed as he caught me wincing when I lifted one of the heavy backpacks to load in the back of the van. "You okay?"

"Oh yeah. Just overextended my shoulder a little bit. Nothing to worry about."

Wade nodded. "Well, no sense in making it worse. Let me deal with the rest of these bags."

"He caught me right when I was about to slip on the trail. It was a dicey spot," the woman chimed in. "If I'd slipped further, I would've fallen over the edge of the trail. It wasn't life-threatening, but I'm definitely glad he caught me."

She smiled brightly at me, and I shrugged. "That's why I was there."

In short order, we were on the way back to the lodge. I was annoyed as hell with myself. All I could think about was how soon I would see Shay. Fuck me.

It had rained most of the morning, and I was damp and ready for a shower. Cranky as I was, I didn't intend to grab dinner with the rest of the crew at the lodge.

Once we got back and the guests headed to their rooms, Wade looked my way. "I'm not asking about your shoulder now, but you okay?" he asked.

I didn't want to contemplate how obvious it was that I was out of sorts. "Yeah. Just a little tired and sore."

I wasn't about to offer up that I was beyond frustrated with Shay setting up house in my brain. There were lots of reasons why I shouldn't allow what happened with her last week to happen again. There were just as many reasons why I shouldn't even consider a serious relationship.

It wasn't just Shay, though, it was the myriad of complications that came with her. She was my best friend's little sister. Not to mention, she'd been through some heavy shit. We both had baggage. She deserved a man...well, a man not like me. I had my own demons to fight.

Wade was distracted when someone called over from the staff area. His head whipped around. Because it was Dani. It was no secret to the rest of us he and Dani had a thing for each other. Yet, both of them were stubbornly ignoring it.

I loved to tease him about it, though. "You go check with your girlfriend. I'm gonna skip dinner here tonight. I need a hot shower and to crash soon as possible."

"All right, man. Shay's down here, by the way. In case you were wondering," he said, promptly getting me back for my dig about Dani.

"Touché," I replied with a grin, recalling his observations about Shay and me the other day.

"Need a ride up there?"

"Nah, I can handle it." I lifted my backpack with my good arm and waved as I turned toward the farmhouse, walking along the well-worn path through the trees.

I didn't even want to think about the fact that when Wade mentioned Shay was down at the lodge for dinner, I was so fucking tempted to stay. Just to see her.

I told myself it was for the best she was there. I would shower, scrounge something up for dinner, and then be in my room by the time she got back.

A scalding hot, soothing shower later, I made my way into the kitchen at the farmhouse. I slapped together two sandwiches and ate them in the quiet of the kitchen, laughing when I heard Squeaky at the door. I let her in, greeting her with an apple slice and a few strokes on her back. That was all she needed before heading back outside.

Glancing up at the clock above the sink, I saw it was going on nine p.m. My plan to basically escape from Shay by hiding in my room wasn't working out. I told myself it was rude not to say hello. I didn't know when she'd be back, but I found myself lingering.

Just as I was giving myself a little lecture, I heard the front door open. The sound of it closing echoed down the hallway in the quiet farmhouse. I heard a soft shuffling and figured she was taking her boots off by the door.

In a moment, she appeared in the archway into the kitchen. Fuck me. She was so damn beautiful. With her honey gold hair pulled up in a messy ponytail and her cheeks flushed from the cool evening air, she was simply breathtaking.

"Hey," she said softly.

"Hey."

She stepped into the kitchen, and my eyes soaked up the sight of her. She wore a cotton skirt. The stretchy fabric clung to her hips and then flared around her ankles. There was nothing remarkable about it. Atop that, she wore a loose blouse with tiny buttons running up the center and a silky tie at the top. The scoop-neck tempted my eyes to linger on the soft curves of her breasts just above.

She wore a pair of hot pink socks, which made me smile. I didn't realize I was staring until my eyes made their way back into her face and noticed her cheeks were flushed.

"How was the trip?" she asked.

It was a perfectly reasonable and expected question, seeing as I had just returned from a trip. Yet, if I were to answer truthfully, I would've said that it sucked. Because I couldn't stop thinking about her, and I'd been impatient to get back to her the entire time.

I shouldn't have been thinking any of those thoughts because she wasn't someone I could let myself want.

As if to emphasize a point, my cock swelled. Because she

was so damn beautiful and the chemistry between us was so damn powerful, my body couldn't *not* respond.

"Jackson?"

Shay's question broke through my train of thought. I realized I hadn't even answered her first question. "I'm fine. And the trip was fine. How was dinner?"

"Delicious, but I've noticed when it comes to Dani's cooking, it's always delicious. Oh wait, I brought you leftovers. I left them on the table by the door."

She spun away. Of course, all I could notice was the nice view of her ass. The way the cotton skirt hugged her curves was not convenient for the state of my body.

Within seconds, she was back, handing over one of the paper takeout boxes from the lodge. As I reached to get it, reflexively using my right arm, I flinched slightly.

"Are you okay?" she asked.

Next thing I knew, she was beside me, her hand gliding lightly over my shoulder. "Wade mentioned you hurt your shoulder. He said you were being a man about it." She still had the takeout box in hand and turned to set it on the table beside us. "Let me take a look."

I heard my breath draw in sharply. Having Shay this close was dangerous. Three days of missing her, three days of replaying our last encounter in the barn, three days of reminding myself why I couldn't have her, and my body was in out-and-out opposition.

No matter how many times I told myself I shouldn't, and couldn't, want her, my body had a different opinion and was definitely winning the argument.

Ever since I came back from the war, I'd been quite reasonable about relationships. I was crystal clear on the fact that wanting anything more than a basic arrangement where mutual needs were satisfied was a bad plan. So far, I had no trouble keeping those lines clear in my head. With Shay, everything blurred.

If she noticed how I was reacting to her touch, she didn't

let on. Her hand curved over my shoulder, pausing right where it was sore and tight in the front. "Give me just a few minutes to get that tension out," she murmured softly. "Sit down."

I found myself obeying. Sitting down in one of the chairs by the table, I closed my eyes, telling myself that this was impersonal and it would help my shoulder. I was shirtless, wearing nothing but jeans. Because, of course, I had my grand plan, the one where I got to my bedroom before she got home. So much for that.

She probed gently at first. When I let out a soft sigh, she asked, "It's sore right here, isn't it?"

"That's the spot. I just overextended it. It's tight," I murmured in reply.

"Just tell me if I go too deep, okay?"

Shay couldn't know the double meaning her words carried. While I sensed her answering desire for me was powerful, I didn't think she was wrestling against the same force I was.

I murmured my assent and closed my eyes again. She stood behind me, starting out massaging both shoulders and around the base of my neck. Although her touch was electric, it felt heavenly. A few days of carrying a full backpack would cause tension under any circumstances. Throw in me overextending my shoulder this morning and the tension was bundled in knots. After a few moments, she shifted to stand at my side, sliding her hand carefully over my shoulder. She started on my good shoulder, telling me she was getting a sense of how it should feel.

Dear God, it felt too good. My cock was rock hard. I shifted carefully, relieved I was seated so perhaps my arousal wouldn't be visible.

She shifted to my other side, standing almost in front of me. "Oh wow, it's really tight here. What did you do?" she asked as her fingers probed gently into the tight, sore spot at the juncture where my arm joined my shoulder.

I had to focus to answer, trying to ignore the scent of her winding itself around me. "Well, it started to rain on the hike down. One of the women slipped on a rock. I reached out to grab her because we were right near the edge of the trail. Nothing major, but I overextended it."

"Oh, I'll say. You'll need to take it easy for a few days," Shay murmured.

I figured this was some sort of torture. I had no clue what I did to deserve it. It felt so damn good to have her massaging away the tension. I knew it would still be sore, but I also had enough sense to know this would keep it from getting much worse. As good as it felt, my body was on fire, taut with need for her.

The rain had stopped this evening. Yet, Shay still carried its scent on her, the earthy, rich scent of rain in the spring—new grass, sunshine, and her, mingled with the subtle scent of leather.

Dammit all to hell. The scent of leather was usually soothing for me. Because it meant I was either about to go riding, or work with one of the horses, which was something I loved, something which brought me peace, no matter what else was going on in my life. Now, that scent was all tangled up in Shay, in the feel of her slick, wet pussy clenching around my fingers as she flew apart in the tack room.

She made a soft sound, and my eyes flew open. She wasn't doing anything to be purposefully seductive, but then Shay—all by herself, with no effort, no artifice—was a seduction.

Her hand stopped its motion, resting on my shoulder. "Is that too much?" she asked.

I shook my head wordlessly. My eyes snagged on her mouth — her gorgeous, fucking sexy as hell mouth. As we stared at each other, it felt as if the air itself was filled with sparks, each one feeding into another.

My eyes, my greedy eyes, dipped down. I noticed the wild beat of her pulse along the soft skin of her neck, and followed the curve of her blouse to that little tie at the top, nothing more than two strips of silk and buttons underneath that I wanted to tear open.

It didn't skip my attention that her nipples were hard, pressing against the thin cotton. A wave of satisfaction rolled through me. If I was going to be this helpless in the face of my need for her, I could at least take comfort that perhaps—maybe, just maybe—she was fighting the same battle.

My eyes made their way back up to her face to find her cheeks flushed and her mossy green eyes darkening. "It's not too much," I belatedly said. "Feels much better now."

I was sternly trying to tell myself I should stand up and walk out of the room. Right now.

That voice was distant and weak. Hell, it might as well have been miles away. Shay started to step back, perhaps in an effort to save me from myself.

My arm moved of its own accord, slipping around her waist and pulling her between my knees. Sweet fucking hell. I had Shay right where I wanted her. With me seated and her standing, her eyes were level with mine, her lips mere inches away.

"What are you doing, Jackson?" she whispered.

"*This*," I replied. Keeping one hand where it landed, on the sweet curve of her ass, I lifted the other and caught the end of the silky tie on her blouse, tugging it loose. I watched as it fell open, just enough to tempt me beyond all reason.

Chapter Fourteen

SHAY

"This."

The moment Jackson said that single word, he tugged lightly at the tie on my blouse. The top fell open, and he dipped his head, placing a kiss right between the valley of my breasts.

That single kiss was so hot, it radiated through my entire body, pinwheels of sensation spinning wildly and sending tingles straight through me.

When I came home tonight and saw him standing barefoot in the kitchen, in nothing but a pair of jeans, his glorious chest bare for me to see, I nearly melted on the spot. Perhaps the only thing that prevented it was the many lectures I'd given myself periodically over the last few days in his absence. I'd reminded myself of all the reasons why it probably wasn't smart—in fact, it was incredibly stupid—to want him this much.

Yet, my reminders were to no avail. Not when the attraction between us seemed to override every single ounce of common sense. My crazy impulses couldn't be buttoned up and shut down.

Maybe it wasn't smart, but I wanted – oh, how I wanted —to lose myself in Jackson. To forget the baggage I carried with me, and to forget the scars, most of them hidden on my psyche and on my heart.

I wasn't looking for love—that was far too much to ask from the universe, as far as I was concerned. If all I took away from this was one crazy night, perhaps it would be a memory to replace the rest.

The loose tie allowed my blouse to fall open a little, but not too much. Tremors ran through me and a sheen of perspiration bloomed on my skin. His lips pressed another kiss, incrementally lower.

Compared to Jackson, I wasn't very tall. With him seated, his head was just barely lower than mine. He looked up, his eyes assessing, measuring. I felt as if he could see right through me. The sensation gave me pause. Because I didn't want anyone to see right through me.

I tried not to think about it very much, but once you've experienced an abusive relationship, you question everything about yourself and feel slightly crazy most of the time. Wanting to shove that feeling away, I sifted my fingers in his hair, leaning down.

"Kiss me."

"I'm busy trying to decide just how bad of an idea this is," he replied.

"I don't have any expectations. This just feels good."

Emotion welled inside, and I tried to tamp it down, to ignore it. True desire was what drove me to this moment, but I couldn't deny that Jackson wasn't just some random man. I'd known him for years. I trusted him. Perhaps that was the most important factor. I decided abruptly I didn't care to know why I was ignoring all the reasons why this was a bad idea.

He studied me. I became acutely aware of the feel of his palm cupping the bottom of my ass, his fingers teasing right along the crease between my thighs. Though his mind might've been thinking this was a bad idea, his hands clearly had a different opinion.

His other hand had fallen to the dip of my waist. He moved, sliding over the curve of my hip in a soothing pass. "I know," he belatedly replied.

"Then kiss me."

I leaned slightly forward as he angled up, and our lips collided. This time, it didn't start slow. It started fierce and got even fiercer in a hot second. His tongue swept into my mouth as his hand slid up under my shirt, the calloused surface sending a prickle of goose bumps over my skin.

He worked my mouth like magic. Dear God, Jackson could kiss, so good it was downright dangerous. Seductive bites, deep sweeps of his tongue as he worked my mouth with his, nearly devouring me. I loved every second of it. It was hot, wet, deep, and intense. I could forget everything when I was at the mercy of his mouth. His hand traveled slowly over the curve of my belly, cupping a breast and rolling his thumb across the tight, aching peak of my nipple. With a flick of his thumb at the clasp between my breasts, they tumbled loose, and I nearly cried out when he transferred his attention to my other breast, lightly pinching the nipple.

All the while, we just kept kissing. Unlike the other day in the tack room, it wasn't a rushed frenzy. Oh, it was hot, but Jackson seemed to be taking his sweet time.

When I shifted my legs where I stood between his knees, my knee brushing across the hard evidence of his arousal, a flicker of fear danced along the edges of my mind. It startled me, and I stiffened up for a minute, suddenly becoming aware of where I was and what I was doing. The last time I had actual sex, Clint raped me. And nearly beat me to death in the aftermath.

I masked my sudden tension by flinging myself into our kiss, spearing my fingers through Jackson's shaggy curls. Tears pricked at the corners of my eyes. I hadn't expected this, but I should've known better. The other day in the tack room had been such an explosion, it overrode all of my defensive impulses.

I was almost frantic now, desperate to capture that feeling of being lost in nothing but a tide of need, sensation, and desire, obliterating all the bad memories. I moved to straddle his lap, deliberately pushing myself up against the edges of my fear.

Jackson was strong, most definitely stronger than me. His grip tightened on my hip, holding me in place.

"If I'm gonna make a crazy decision," he murmured as he drew away from my lips, "it won't be a rushed fuck in the kitchen."

I was still reeling, shaky, twisted, and tossed asunder inside with sensation battling against a tiny flicker of a bad memory. It was a powerful one, though, and carried heavy shadows with it.

"Okay," I managed in reply, my voice a little ragged. I hoped against hope that if he picked up on it, he chalked it up to the desire leaving me rattled.

He moved smoothly, pushing the chair back as he stood before lifting me in his arms. I was so startled, I laughed. "You're carrying me?" I asked, angling my face to look at him.

"I am."

Jackson held me easily, one hand under my bottom and the other under my knees. I didn't mind the close encounter with his chest. Not one bit. I turned my head, unable to resist dusting a few kisses along the surface. His skin was warm and a rich amber. He was a man who spent most of his hours outdoors, the sun burnishing him all over.

The incongruity of the moment nudged me out of the intrusion of fear. He moved quickly, striding up the stairs, carrying me as easily as if he were carrying a child.

It was strange. His strength should've frightened me, but it was Jackson, and I knew I could trust him.

When we reached the hallway upstairs, he shouldered through his bedroom door just as I began to wonder where he meant to take me. I hadn't even been in here, so I looked around curiously as he eased me down at the foot of the bed. The upstairs of the farmhouse had angled ceilings, and all the walls were painted a soft gray. The hardwood floors gleamed. There was a door to one side that I presumed led to the master bathroom.

A king-size bed sat in the center of the room with tables on either side. It was clearly an antique with rich mahogany posts at each corner. It had a lovely, stately quality to it.

"White doesn't really seem to be your color," I observed as I took in the pristine white down quilt atop the bed, with matching pillows piled high against the wooden headboard.

Jackson chuckled and lifted a shoulder in a shrug. "Ash decorated the room. She decorated the whole house, but I bet you could've guessed that."

He moved smoothly, stepping to me and swiftly undoing the buttons below the open tie on my blouse. "Now, where were we?" he murmured as he leaned down, laving his tongue over my tight nipple.

The sensation of pleasure was sharp and acute. It spun through me, swirling into the ache building between my thighs. I gasped when he shifted his attention, the suction gentle on my other nipple. This, *this* might make me forget.

My blouse and bra fell to the floor when his hands swept over my shoulders. I barely noticed him smooth my skirt over my hips until it fell in a rumple around my feet. When he straightened, I could feel the searing heat of his gaze as his eyes traveled over me.

"You're so fucking gorgeous," he said, his voice low, the gruff sound of it sending a prickle of awareness down my spine and goose bumps chasing over my skin.

I didn't know if any man had ever told me I was beautiful. If they had, I had forgotten it. It was buried under the mountains of self-recrimination in the aftermath of a man who took me apart piece by piece.

I flushed all over. Blessedly, Jackson didn't appear to expect me to say anything. Seeing as I couldn't find words, that was a relief. Closing the distance between us, the backs of his fingers trailed over my breasts and down across my belly. I was drenched in arousal.

"Hmm. All for me," he murmured.

His fingers teased over the damp silk between my thighs. He slipped a single finger under the edge of the silk, dragging it through my slick folds. I cried out. Just like he'd done in the tack room, he drew his hand away and tasted my arousal on his fingers.

Jackson never once broke eye contact with me, and I had to fight to keep control. I didn't know if it was possible to climax from a look alone, but I supposed I might be about to find out. In a flash, he lifted me again, laying me down on the bed. He stretched out beside me, propping himself up on an elbow.

His eyes were intent, sweeping over my body as he began to drive me to madness with his lips, teeth, and tongue.

My body was humming, restless and near frantic, with need spreading through me like fire. I didn't know if I could bear Jackson's slow, teasing exploration of my body.

In a distant corner of my mind was also that tiny flicker of fear, a fear I hadn't even known was still holding onto me. I thought maybe if I could lasso this wild, thrumming attraction between us, I could barrel through it and get to the other side.

Jackson's palm slid over my belly, his touch sure, smooth and languid. He was in no hurry. His lips dusted hot kisses along my collarbone, dipping down to capture one of my nipples. I cried out, the pleasure sharp with an incremental edge of pain to it that fed into the desire storming through me.

I was slick with need, shifting my legs restlessly as his

hand slid down to cup my mound, his fingers pressing against the damp silk. My hips bucked into his touch, and I gasped his name.

He hooked his fingers over the edge of my panties and dragged them off swiftly before proceeding to make me forget everything but the hot, dark, delicious feel of his touch. His fingers teased over my folds. One finger slid inside me, my channel clenching around him instantly. He murmured something against my skin as he shifted, moving down my body, his lips blazing a fiery trail over my belly, my entire body rippling with hot shivers. Tremors rocked me when he slid another finger inside me, pumping lightly.

"Jackson, I need..." I gasped, my words becoming incoherent as he stretched me with a deep stroke.

"Oh, we're not rushing this," he murmured as his weight shifted, and I felt the bulk of his shoulders press my knees apart. With the weight of my prior sexual experiences bearing down upon me—not counting what had happened with Jackson within the last week, which was the most intense sexual experience of my life, even though it hadn't been the full act—I felt suddenly vulnerable and exposed.

A sound of protest escaped. Not because I wanted him to stop. Rather because, somehow, I'd gotten this far in life without ever having a man pleasure me this way. I fell back into the pillows, and I felt him lift his head.

"Yes?" he asked, the word coming out slowly as my sex clenched, and I felt the juices of my arousal on the insides of my thighs.

Dragging my eyes open, I tried to catch my breath, but all I could manage was a shallow gasp. "I've never..." My words ran out as a flush heated my cheeks. He was quiet, waiting and watching, making me nearly frantic with his fingers as he stroked through my slick folds.

"Never what?" he prompted as he sank a finger inside me again, my hips reflexively arching into his touch.

"Had anyone do...that," I mumbled, biting back a moan.

With my sexual experiences limited to one man, a man entirely uninterested in my pleasure, I'd never experienced oral sex beyond being the one giving it. I didn't want to explain any of that and hoped Jackson would just drop it.

He dropped it all right, just not quite how I expected. "Well then, you have to try it," he murmured, a sly grin curling the corner of his mouth.

"Jackson, I..."

Just as I was fighting my anxiety, he licked into my core, the sensation so acute and so gentle at once that I almost came instantly. With his skillful fingers sliding in and out and his tongue teasing me languidly, I was nearly incoherent with need, chasing after a sweet release.

I lost sense of time, place, everything—everything but the feel of Jackson's mouth, tongue, and fingers pushing me closer and closer to the edge. A wave of pressure gathered inside. When I cried out, he caught my clit with his lips, giving it the slightest bit of suction. Pleasure shot through me, the wave cresting and crashing through my body in ripples.

Dragging my eyes open with my breath coming in ragged rasps, I watched Jackson rise up. With the soft glow of the lamp, his muscled form was cast in shadow. He tugged his jeans and briefs down, his cock springing free.

Although I was boneless from pleasure, the tremors of my climax still pinging through me, I tensed when I saw him. He was quite well-endowed, his cock long and thick. I fought against the sense of tension mingling with the after-shocks. I didn't need sex to be forever ruined by my ex.

Jackson abruptly turned, striding to the bathroom. "Hey..." I began to say.

"Condom," came his one-word reply tossed over his shoulder.

In a matter of seconds, he was stepping back into the bedroom. There was something so damn sexy about the way he looked at me—his gaze dark and intent, a searing tenderness contained within. Although that tiny fear was hanging on in the background, desire was too. Because I wanted to feel him against me, to feel him filling me.

The mattress dipped with his weight as he stretched out beside me. I had expected him to instantly chase after his own pleasure. When he didn't, I was flummoxed, thrown off. The moment I rolled my head to the side, his lips descended over mine. His kiss was lazy, seductive bites, hungry and sweet.

I felt suspended in a hazy, searing hot, sensual exploration. Once again, that old fear rattled when I felt the brush of his arousal against my thigh. I told myself I could ignore it, that Jackson could make me forget everything.

Then, he shifted his weight, and I felt the hard, heavy length of his cock pressing insistently against my hip, and my body reacted. I flinched and tensed instantly. He froze.

Chapter Fifteen

SHAY

"Don't stop," I blurted out, rolling toward him. Unfortunately, that brought me into contact with his cock all over again. All of my muscles tensed. It was clear my body had a hold on what was happening. Seeing as this was the very first time I tried to have sex since I'd been raped, and I'd only had sex with one man—a violent, abusive man—I didn't have a roadmap for this.

I couldn't have known the mere attempt to have sex would trigger me. In no way was what was happening with Jackson anything like sex with Clint, beyond the basic mechanics of it.

There had been no kissing and no foreplay with Clint. Plain old sex with Clint was a constant letdown for him where he berated me for not being experienced enough, for not relaxing, and so on. Even discounting the time he raped me, I didn't have a reservoir of good sexual experiences to override those memories. It all ended with raw power shoving me down and forcing me to endure a rough assault.

I swallowed, holding still and praying for Jackson to just ignore this.

"Shay?"

Jackson's hand stilled, although he didn't pull away. The feel of it was warm on my skin. I opened my eyes to find his gaze waiting. The heat was still banked in his eyes, but the air around us had shifted. I could feel questions tumbling through his mind.

"What?"

"You're tense," he answered, his tone level.

Emotion was thick in my throat and tears pressed hot in my eyes. To my mortification, I was afraid I was about to burst into tears in front of Jackson at the absolute worst time I could imagine. I tried to swallow through it. I managed to not cry, but when he shifted slightly, and I felt the length of him against my leg, my body went rigid once again.

Unfortunately, Jackson knew me well. He drew away slightly. "What the hell is going on, Shay?"

I shook my head wildly. "It's just been a while."

He was quiet, his gaze assessing. "Maybe it's been a while, but something's up. You're tense as hell. You flinched three times. I don't know what the hell is going on, but I'm not an idiot. We can stop this now. If you're having second thoughts, maybe that's for the best. This is crazy anyway."

I was suddenly frantic, almost desperate to not let my past tangle into my present like this and ruin my one attempt to replace the bad memories.

"It's not that! It's just, well, the last time I had sex, Clint raped me," I blurted out.

Oh fuck. Of all the things I meant to say, *that* definitely wasn't something I wanted Jackson to know. Even Remy didn't know this part of the whole mess.

Jackson's eyes widened, his breath drawing in sharply. The air around us felt heavy. "I'll fucking kill him," he said savagely.

"I'm sorry. I should've told you. I guess I didn't think it mattered. Everything felt so good. I thought..."

Jackson started to shake his head, clearly concerned with my response. "What the hell are you apologizing for? It's not your fault."

His words stopped as he looked at me. I wished I could read into what he was thinking. I couldn't. "I think maybe we should give this a rain check," he finally said.

"No!" I shifted toward him again. "I don't want to stop. I want you. Don't even try to pretend you don't want me," I murmured.

Jackson had started to move away from me, and as I moved quickly in his direction, I ending up sitting astride him. I hadn't planned it that way, but I landed right over his hips, my wet, highly-sensitized core sliding over his hard, hot length. I felt his arousal pulse, and he gripped my hips tightly, an expression bordering on pain crossing his face.

"Shay," he said, his tone laced with warning.

"What? So what if I had some shitty stuff happen? I'm fine."

My hips rocked on their own, and I suddenly realized the triggering fear that had struck me was already passing. Perhaps because I was the one on top and felt in control. I also had no fear of Jackson.

He simply stared at me, his grip still tight on my hips. Although I couldn't tell precisely what he was thinking, it was clear he didn't know what the hell to do.

He closed his eyes, leaning his head back into the pillows, his chest rising and falling with a deep breath. That had the unintended side effect of a ripple of motion in his hips, his cock moving slightly. It felt good, so good. I was suddenly almost giddy. Whatever shifted had pushed me through to the other side of the twinge of fear.

This was Jackson. I knew he would never hurt me, not like Clint. I also knew that once I was lost in sensation with him, the pleasure would take over.

He opened his eyes. "Look, Shay, this was already a crazy decision for both of us. I'm not gonna lie and try to pretend

I don't want you. But, I don't think it's a good idea for us to let this keep going."

"I do." I nudged him lightly with my palm on his chest. "It's just sex. You'd be doing me a favor. I'm not tense now, I swear. See," I said for emphasis, rocking my hips slightly, my pussy sliding over the underside of his cock.

His breath came out in a hiss. He closed his eyes again, his entire body tightening as he gripped my hips to hold me still.

"I'd be doing you a favor?" he muttered, as he dragged his eyes open again.

"Yes. I don't have any expectations. Whatever it is, it's just sex. I don't want to go through the rest of my life with my last sexual experience being…" I let my words trail off because I didn't want to say the words again.

I couldn't even believe this conversation was happening. But once the truth came out, well, it was out. In a way, I was immensely relieved. At least, I could just lay that ugly part of my past on the table and let it be known.

I also knew the chemistry burning between Jackson and me was rare, and I wanted to take advantage of it. Because I knew if it wasn't this hot, my memories would get in the way. I also didn't know how I could ever trust another man. Jackson came with something like a trust guarantee.

He was my older brother's best friend, totally reliable, and a good man. I was at no risk of harm at his hands. Plus, he kissed like a dream and he'd twice now sent me flying into the most intense orgasms of my life.

With Jackson simply staring at me, I rocked my hips again, letting out a little sigh at the point of contact when my swollen clit rubbed his hard cock.

He shook his head slowly. "This is crazy."

"We're past crazy."

I decided not to wait and rose up slightly, sliding my palm around his cock, feeling a smile curl my lips when it swelled further at my touch. I kept expecting him to try to talk me out of it again, so I moved fast. For a flash, a memory struck when I remembered the last time a man had been inside of me. It dissipated quickly, a distant, detached flicker. Then, I was sinking down around him, the stretch of him filling me.

Jackson didn't move, although I could feel his cock pulsing inside of me when I settled myself down. Perhaps it was because it was Jackson and I knew I could trust him, or perhaps it was because the desire was so powerful it took over everything, but I felt no fear. Nothing but pure pleasure and a surge of power from Jackson.

Shay sank down slowly, her hair in a tousle around her face, her green eyes bright in the dim light of my bedroom. With her dusky pink nipples right in front of me, it was all I could do not to lean up and suck one right into my mouth again. She settled her hips over mine, a little hum of satisfaction coming from her throat. She was wet and tight and felt like heaven.

I was stunned, unsure how we got to this point. I knew when she flinched that something was wrong, but I was entirely unprepared for what she told me.

This was more than crazy. And yet somehow, I couldn't stop it even when my mind told me I should. My body, of course, was downright insistent. Buried deeply in her slick, pulsing channel, I was near drunk from the sensation of her. I was barely hanging onto my control. Once we passed this point with me inside of her, I was going to let her set the pace.

Her hand trailed down my chest. Slivers of fire chased in the wake of her touch. She shifted her hips, and I felt the squeeze of her around me. She was relaxed, her eyes on mine. She lifted a hand to cup one of her breasts, teasing the tight bead of her nipple.

"Fuck, Shay. You make me crazy. You have no idea how beautiful you are."

She didn't reply, biting her lip. "Don't make me do all the work," she murmured with a slow grin.

"This is all you, darlin'." I flexed my hips, savoring her low moan and the clench of her pussy around my cock.

I would let her set the pace, but I'd be damned if she didn't come out of this without another climax. I wanted to give her a thousand to make up for whatever the hell else her ex had put her through.

She settled into a rhythm, rocking slowly. I eased my grip on one of her hips, sliding my palm up her spine as I shifted on the pillows, sitting up halfway. I wanted to feel her against me, and I knew this angle would give her the friction to fly apart.

She settled in easily, sighing with delight when I arched into her. With her breasts rubbing against my chest, I dusted kisses on her neck, savoring the salty tang of her skin. At this angle, I could feel her tighten quickly. I reached between us, pressing my thumb over her clit and watching as she arched back with a rough cry, her pussy clamping down and milking my release from me. It was an intense, almost painfully sharp climax as it whipped through me.

I hadn't meant to call her name, but it came out in a rush with a shuddered groan. She relaxed against me, tucking her head into my neck. She breathed deeply, little tremors running through her body.

I meant to find a way to untangle myself from Shay. There was only one problem. I didn't want to.

This had gone from a bad idea, to a crazy idea, to a complicated mess.

Somewhere between telling myself I should slide out from under her and somehow shift the tone of this encounter, I fell asleep. Deep in the night, I woke with her warm against me. I'd slid out from inside of her, but she was still there, naked and curled up against my side with one of her legs thrown over mine. Her breath came in soft, steady gusts against my shoulder, and I had my arm wrapped around her back with my palm cupping her sweet ass.

That would've been the point where I knocked some sense into myself. Yet, I had slept more deeply for those last few hours than I had in years. I rolled out from under her carefully, stepping into the bathroom to very belatedly dispose of the condom that must've fallen off after I slipped out of her.

Closing the door, I flicked on the light and splashed water on my face. My hair stuck up in spikes. As I stared at myself, I noticed the lines of tension that usually bracketed my face had dissolved. I didn't want to think too much. Between the intensity of our encounter and the shattering news she had shared, thinking wasn't something I wanted to do just now.

Turning the light off, I returned to the bedroom. Moonlight fell through the tall windows flanking the bed. Shay was cast in a silvery glow. Considering I couldn't even talk myself into walking downstairs to crash on the couch, I certainly didn't have the heart to bundle her off the bed and carry her to her bedroom.

I didn't seem to have much willpower when it came to her, especially not in those hours of the night that were usually lonely and restless. I found myself carefully easing under the covers and pulling her into my arms again. She shifted against me with a soft sigh, burrowing her head against my neck.

In spite of everything, in spite of the tangled complications that were bound to ensue, it felt so damn *good* to hold her in my arms. It felt good and right.

———

The following day, the morning at the farmhouse was cloaked in a strange sense of comfort. I had expected to be out of sorts, but I had slept so incredibly well, I felt rested in a way I hadn't been in too damn long. Shay, well, she was easy to be around. I woke to the sound of the shower running in the bathroom off the side of my bedroom. I kicked the covers off, intending to climb in there with her, only to hear the water turn off before my feet even hit the floor.

As I sat halfway up against the pillows, debating what to do, she came out, rubbing her hair with a towel and wrapped in a white, fluffy robe. She looked over at me, and for a moment, the air felt electrified when our eyes collided. Then, she smiled.

"Morning. I already started coffee. I hope you don't mind I used the shower," she said, gesturing with her thumb over her shoulder. "You neglected to mention the hot water pressure is much better in here."

"I didn't know. I don't use the other shower."

With a last rub of the towel in her hair, she let her arm fall, looping the towel over her forearm. "Well, take my word for it. It's better."

Then, she turned and walked out of my bedroom. Meanwhile, if my cock could have spoken, it would have shouted for her to return posthaste.

Fuck. There was stupid, and there was what happened last night. I knew my attraction to Shay danced along the edge of dangerous. Yet, I hadn't counted on the way it would feel to be with her.

I listened as she returned to her bedroom, and moments later, the sound of her footsteps moving down the hallway and the stairs. I stood and strolled into the shower. I couldn't take it and found myself forced to take matters into my own hands, or show up downstairs, rock hard and ready.

As promised, coffee was ready when I made it downstairs. Shay looked up from the counter where she was whisking eggs in a bowl. "I thought I'd make scrambled eggs. Is that okay?"

Even when Ash was here, she didn't cook. That was a joke about my sister. She hated cooking. I had declared many times she would need to find a man who could feed her. Being used to fending for myself, it was unaccountably nice to have Shay offering to make breakfast.

"Of course it's okay." I stepped to the counter and poured a cup of coffee. I took a sip, savoring the rich, dark flavor. "You make damn good coffee," I said, turning and resting my hips against the counter.

She glanced over with a smile. "I love coffee, so it better be good."

Beyond the visceral memories bombarding me of what it felt like to have her naked in my arms and the way she looked as she arched back in the throes of pleasure, one memory kept striking hard. I didn't know what the hell to do with what she told me last night. I was floundering in a way I never had before.

I considered myself a straightforward man, preferring to tackle difficult subjects directly. After I got back from the war, my therapist had even commented on my tendency to walk straight up to the most painful topics first—metaphorically speaking, of course.

For the first time in a long time, I found myself struggling with how to approach the topic. Shay saved me the trouble.

She cast a careful glance my way. "I can practically feel you worrying over there. I'm sure you're freaking out about what I told you last night. Please don't. I'm just a statistic. It's certainly nothing to obsess over."

Despite her words, I could see the tension in her shoulders and practically feel her body vibrating from a few feet away. I moved on instinct, not really thinking. Setting my coffee down, I pushed away from the counter and walked up behind her. I slid a hand down her shoulder and stepped close behind her, resting my chin in the crook of her neck. With one hand on her hip, I curled the other around her waist and pulled her flush against me. "You're not a statistic, Shay. Not to me. Not to anyone who cares about you."

I wasn't sure what she expected, but I didn't think that was it. Her breath drew in sharply, and I felt a fine tremor running through her. I knew she was crying.

Sweet Jesus. There were a lot of things I knew how to deal with, but Shay crying over her ex raping her wasn't one of them.

"Oh shit, don't cry," I heard myself saying, my voice gruffer than I intended.

She took a deep breath, letting it out with a ragged sigh as she stirred the scrambled eggs. "Okay, I need you to maybe not do that," she said softly.

"Not do what?" I asked, as my palm rubbed in a slow circle on her hip.

"Hold me like that, and be all nice," she mumbled.

I sensed her spark returning. It felt as if she were calling upon it purposefully. Yet, I didn't know the right thing to do.

"Maybe I want to," I finally said.

Hell if I knew why, but that got a chuckle from her. With a last stir of the eggs, she adjusted the heat to low and turned in my arms.

I had no fucking map for how to make sense of this. It was bad enough that I just had the best sex of my life with my best friend's little sister. Even worse, I knew it could be nothing more than that because I was no candidate for a relationship. I had too much baggage. Throw in what had happened to Shay, and I had absolutely no clue what to do. All I knew was last night I felt like we were in it too deeply for me to think. When she yanked the reins out of my hands, I had lost all control of the situation at that point.

I preferred to chalk it up to out-of-control lust at that point, but I knew there was more than that between us. *And therein lies the problem.*

Shay lifted a hand, smoothing the damp hair along my hairline. "Let me make you breakfast and let's try to be normal this morning," she said, shimmying out from between the stove and me. I resisted the urge to reach for her and pull her back into my arms.

Clinging to what little sanity I had, I turned and picked up my coffee. I got two plates out of the cabinet, and within a few minutes, we were seated at the table across from each other. The eggs were delicious, of course. We ate quietly, and blessedly, it wasn't awkward or tense.

After we finished eating, I pushed my plate away and looked over at her. On the heels of a fortifying sip of coffee, I asked, "Does Remy know?"

A subtle thread of tension snapped through the air. Shay set her fork down and took a measured swallow of coffee before answering. "No. Obviously he knows some, but not all of it. Clint was convicted of aggravated assault. I didn't tell anyone he raped me."

Anger spun tight inside, a sense of raw fury slicing through me. It wasn't that I hadn't known the outlines of what happened. Hell, it was splashed all over the news. Son of a wealthy politician and all that. It was ugly. North Carolina wasn't that small of a state, population-wise, but word traveled for high-profile stories, and that one had all the grabby headlines. Assault. Speculation about whether he actually did it, despite the fact there were witnesses, photographs, and distant video from someone's phone. A DUI crash a few weeks later, and then more stories. I didn't even want to know what else was missing from the news.

I was used to keeping my emotions in check. Hell, I had a few years of solid practice with it. But this? *This* tore me up inside. I wanted to track the guy down and wipe him off the face of the earth.

"It's a damn good thing he's in prison. If I could get my hands on him, I'd fucking kill him," I said flatly.

Shay's skin blanched, but her expression stayed

controlled. "He's not worth it. I don't need anybody fighting a battle for me, only to get themselves in trouble. He got a fifteen-year sentence because of the DUI, so he won't be anywhere near me for a long time."

My fury didn't abate, yet I knew that wasn't what she needed to see.

"It's not your battle to fight, Jackson," she added.

"Fuck, Shay. This isn't about whose battle it is. He raped you. And God knows what else happened before it got to that point."

I saw Shay's hand tighten around the handle of her mug, and took a steadying breath, reminding myself she didn't need to see my fury. "I'm sorry," I finally said, letting my breath out slowly. "I'm just upset about the situation. Why didn't you tell the police he raped you?"

Her shoulders rose and fell with a deep breath, and her throat worked as she swallowed. "Because who was going to believe me? We were together. The only reason the assault charges stuck was because there were witnesses. The neighbor next door saw him go after me outside in the parking lot, and then a few others who were there. They didn't see anything else. That's why I was running out of our condo anyway."

Her words were low and filled with pain. I felt like I was stumbling through a foreign, barren landscape right now. The last few years of my life had been circumscribed by the choices I made. I'd returned home to take over the farm and the projects my father had started before he passed away, every action geared toward finding peace and living in a way where I could keep everything tidy and neat. I wasn't so bad off that I shut the whole world out. But I kept it to friends because those relationships were less complicated, with less potential for emotional landmines and expectations.

This raw lust I felt for Shay rocked me with its intensity. I had thought I could contain it to physical desire only. Last night had proven me wrong on that count, quite spectacularly. And now this, wrapping my brain around the enormity of what actually happened to Shay.

I didn't know why the hell I started this conversation this morning. This urge to comfort her, to protect her, to erase everything that happened to her didn't make sense. Yet, it was so powerful I couldn't ignore it. If Remy knew what happened last night, he would probably gut me alive.

Through the cacophony inside my mind, I took another deep breath and a sip of coffee and nodded. "Okay. I don't really get it, but it's your call."

She shrugged. "There's no point to it now. He's in jail. Trying to bring up this part of it would only drag me through the mud again. We don't have to talk about it. Trust me, I've talked about it plenty in therapy. Now you know the whole truth."

She stood from the table abruptly, collecting her plate and mine, then walking over to the sink. I sat at the table, thinking there were probably still huge gaps in what I knew about what happened and realizing it wasn't fair to her to insist she tell me everything. It was her story to tell, or not, not mine to demand.

"Is it okay if I work with Mischief some this morning?" she asked.

In a way, I was relieved she was so clearly putting the conversation back on safe ground. Yet, there was more, and I knew it. It wasn't about dredging up the details of what happened with her and her ex. It was about the visceral connection between us, and my own past weighing on me and colliding with hers.

"Of course it's okay."

"You have appointments in the office, starting at eight thirty." She put the last plate in the dishwasher and turned to face me as she dried her hands with a dishtowel. "I rearranged your whole schedule," she said, a smile teasing at the corners of her mouth. "You also might find that your office has been organized. Don't blame me, blame Dani."

I stood from the table, fighting the urge to kiss her. I kept it light with a wink and a nod. "The office is all yours, and thank you for dealing with that schedule mess."

At that, I turned and left, thanking God and every other deity I could think of that I had a busy day to maybe, just maybe, keep my mind off of Shay.

Chapter Seventeen

SHAY

Mischief nudged his head against my shoulder, nipping lightly at my sleeve. For a horse, he had little sense of his size. He wiggled his upper lip often, sniffing things out and nudging them constantly. He was an affectionate little guy. Despite his small stature, he had established himself as in charge in the pasture. He appeared to have no sense that he was smaller than every other horse out there, but his attitude made up for it.

I scrubbed behind his ears and unbuckled his bridle. He was accustomed to halters. While a bridle wasn't much different, the bit was a new thing for him. I had elected to start with a rubber snaffle, which turned out to be a good option because he chewed on it constantly.

He was headstrong, but not wild. I imagined he would get accustomed to everything fairly quickly, if only because he was more interested in what was happening around him. He kept chewing on the bit as I gently pulled it out of his mouth.

With a last stroke down his shoulder, I opened the gate

from the enclosed paddock out into the larger pasture. "Go on, buddy."

He lifted his head, his ears perking forward as he looked out toward the rest of the horses who were gathered in a shady area over in the corner. With a flick of his tail, he trotted off. Closing the gate behind him, I looped the bridle over my shoulder and picked up the saddle blanket off the fence where I had left it earlier.

Working with Mischief and the rescue animals was bringing me a sense of peace I had thought elusive for the last few years. As I went to return the bridle to the tack room and the familiar scent struck me, my mind spun back to last week and my first heated encounter with Jackson. Obviously, I hadn't planned on it, but what happened in here had imprinted that scent in my brain, permanently linking it to Jackson.

The door in here had springs on it, so it shut automatically behind me. I took a moment to lean against it, taking several deep breaths in the quiet, private room. Last night had spiraled wildly out of control, far more quickly than I had anticipated.

I didn't regret it. In fact, I adamantly refused to regret it, no matter what the future brought. I finally had a memory to replace all the bad ones. Jackson didn't know this, but I'd only had sex with one other man. I wasn't a prude, but my parents had been high school sweethearts and married after attending college together. Somehow, it had stuck with me that I should try to find the right man. I dated here and there in high school, but not seriously. I never made it to the sex part of things then.

When I was in college and met Clint, he charmed the pants right off of me, literally and figuratively. He was handsome, charming, and well-connected. His father was a politician and his family was quite well-known. There was nothing to set off any of my alarms. The first time he laid his hands on me in violence, my self-esteem had already been shredded by the slow erosion of his strategic verbal and emotional abuse.

Sex had never been anything other than sort of okay at its best for me with Clint. I had chalked it up to my inexperience. I had so desperately wanted to have at least one, just one, sexual experience that wasn't linked to him. I didn't regret that part, not even a little. I also meant what I said to Jackson. I didn't have any expectations. Not a single one.

Yet, that didn't change my emotional train wreck last night. I hadn't meant to blurt out the dark truth of what happened with Clint. I certainly hadn't anticipated the way it would feel to be with Jackson. I had a taste from our encounter here in this room, but nothing more than a glimmer. Something visceral was underneath it, a deep, tugging connection, an electric intimacy.

I needed to find a way to get more sensible. I craved more. After hearing from Dani, I knew Jackson was carrying his own demons. I wished like hell life was a bit more fair. I wished I could expect to fall in love, but I figured my emotional baggage was too heavy. I would take good sex though. In fact, I would take more of it if I could get it.

Later that evening, I finished feeding the animals in the rescue barn, ending my time there by spending a few minutes with Gloria. I'd never spent much time with pigs and had quickly fallen in love with her. She was sweet and affectionate, meandering along behind me as I checked on everyone else.

She had her own space, but we left the door to the stall open because she was such a good girl. Jackson explained to me that she had the run of the barn and the rest of the farm. Without needing to be prompted, she usually curled up and slept in her stall every night. I was quickly getting attached and wanted to ask Jackson if they were looking for a home for her. I certainly hoped not.

"G'night, Gloria," I said, brushing my hand in a smooth stroke down her back. Her skin was warm and a bit prickly with her springy hair. Her curly tail swung in a little circle, and I could've sworn she smiled at me. I didn't really know, but I liked to think she did.

With a last stroke, I straightened and stepped out of her stall. She settled down in a pile of clean straw in the corner. When I stepped out of the barn into the late evening, the sky was stained pink and lavender, the air cooling as the sun slowly slid behind the mountains.

No matter what, these rolling mountains were home to me. Unlike my older brother, I never had the call to travel far and wide. Yet, it was the mountains that felt like home. On evenings like this, a hazy blue could be seen shimmering in the sky above. The rich, earthy scents of the mountains, all the nooks and crannies, the narrow winding roads, and the fresh pine scented air—all of it called to me.

I didn't plan it that way, but I was beyond relieved I had never lived here with Clint. It might've poisoned this place for me. I would've hated the loss, as it would've been yet another hole in my heart.

I walked through the trees between the rescue barn and where the house and horse barn were, reflexively glancing over to the house to see if there were any lights on. I knew Jackson had a full day with vet appointments because I had scheduled them myself. I didn't know if he planned to have dinner at the house, or over at the lodge.

In my week here, I had fallen into the habit of eating at the lodge. As strong as the draw was to go see what he was doing, I didn't want to seem ridiculous. I kept reminding myself again and again and again that I had no expectations. I did *not* need to get caught up in wanting anything from him.

I cut across the small rise to the path that led over to the lodge, smiling at the thought of seeing everyone. I was growing attached to the people here rapidly. I didn't know how long I would be welcome to stay, so I needed to guard against that. I made a mental note to give Ash a call. She had called me the week before I arrived, explaining she would be traveling for a while, but I was welcome to stay as long as I needed.

I couldn't shake the niggling worry that what happened last night might end up setting the wheels in motion for me to leave. No matter what, I needed a place to be. I had lost too much after what happened, and I had nowhere to go, not really. I figured perhaps I could save up a little money over the next few months. If I couldn't stay here, I would find a place somewhere. Most of my friendships had grown distant after everything blew up with Clint. His family had a lot of power and influence, and he had isolated me quite effectively. I had a few friends who maintained tenuous connections with me. Blessedly, Ash was one of them.

A short walk later, I pushed through the back door into the kitchen at the lodge.

"What the hell do you mean?" Dani asked with one hand resting on her hip and a spatula pointing at Wade in the other.

"Oh, for God's sake, Dani, chill out, would you? All I said was I would do the run to Asheville next weekend. I've got a ton of supplies to pick up for the first responder team. Give me a list of what you need, and I'll take care of it."

Dani stared at him, slowly lowering the spatula and turning away. "You better get exactly what I put on the list. The last time you went, you didn't follow instructions well," she called over her shoulder as she returned to something on the stove.

I bit back a laugh. I knew I wasn't the only one who noticed their constant bickering. It didn't seem obvious to Dani, but it was obvious to me there was something between those two. I didn't have the kind of friendship with her yet where I was ready to make that kind of observation.

"Can I help with anything?" I asked as I hung my light-weight jacket on a hook by the door and approached the wide stainless steel table opposite the stove where she was working.

Dani looked up with a smile, blowing a curl out of her eyes. "Nope, I'm all set," she replied as she turned off the burner under a large pan.

"What's for dinner tonight?"

"A giant batch of stir fry. With marinated beef, or tofu, if that's your choice."

"I think you've already figured out I'm not a vegetarian," I returned with a grin.

Glancing to the large table in the back, I saw Jackson at the table, along with a few of the other guys. His back was to me. The moment I saw him, my belly did a little somersault and my pulse picked up its pace. I thought I had done quite well today at keeping myself distracted. I had somehow talked myself into thinking the chemistry didn't burn *that* hot between us, that it was a trick of my memory.

Seeing as nothing more than the sight of his back with his T-shirt stretched over his muscled shoulders and his mussed dark hair was like revving an engine in my body, I supposed I was wrong. Glancing back to Dani, I asked, "Do I need to bring anything over to the table?"

"Wine and beer would be great." She had removed her apron and had two giant platters in her hands.

"That's it?"

"I already got everything else," she called over her shoulder as she strode toward the table in the corner.

I walked over to the large refrigerator at the back, pulling out a six-pack of beer, then reached for two bottles of red wine on the rack beside it. I'd learned this group would usually drink whatever you put in front of them.

I told myself as I was walking over that I wouldn't sit beside Jackson. But, my best-laid plans were all for naught because when I got there, there was nowhere else left to sit. I set the beer and the wine in the center of the table and then climbed over the bench to slide between him and Dawson.

"Hey, darlin'," Dawson said with a wink.

With his shaggy dark blonde hair and his silvery-gray eyes, Dawson was what we called a "looker" around here. And yet, there was no zing for me with him, not even a little. It appeared Jackson was the only man who affected me that way. Surrounded by brawny, sexy men, and not a single one of them set my body alight the way Jackson did.

"Hey, Dawson, how'd your day go?" I asked in return.

Dawson was reaching for a beer and leaning across me to pass one to Jackson. "My day was quite fine. All I did was chop wood. Bored me to tears, but I'm exhausted. After this, I'll probably head into town."

Dani snorted from across the table. "You go to town almost every night." She clucked and shook her head. "You string all those girls along like crazy. You need to man up and just fess up that you never intend to settle down, Dawson. That way, they won't be mooning over you. I had to field a call from a girl here for you just yesterday. She was quite sad you were busy."

"Darlin', I don't lie to anyone," Dawson offered with a wink.

Conversation carried on. Everyone offered their various updates, gleefully interrupting each other. Jackson was quiet beside me, but I could feel the potent heat of him.

I filled a glass of wine for myself and settled in to enjoy yet another scrumptious dinner from Dani. I loved to cook, but damn, she was a miracle worker. Everything she touched was just heavenly. This was a simple dish of egg noodles with a spicy sauce, sautéed onions, and garlic, with crisp vegetables tossed in. Adding in the marinated beef strips made it absolutely yummy.

"Delicious, Dani," I said, catching her eye from across the table and lifting my wine.

She grinned. "I aim to please." Someone else addressed her, and she turned away.

"How was your day?" For a moment, I didn't even realize Jackson was talking to me, but then he nudged me with his knee.

That brief touch sent a zing of electricity sizzling up my thigh and spiraling through me. Glancing to him, not wanting to admit I'd been avoiding looking at him, I met his gaze. Oh. My. God. Just looking at him sent a wash of heat through me, and my pulse took off like a rocket.

I took a sip of my wine before replying. "It was good. Yours?"

"Busy as hell. Someone filled my schedule to the gills," he murmured, his drawl like sweet sorghum. My belly spun, and my breath hitched. I took another sip of wine.

"Well, someone left unexpectedly, putting someone else in the position of rescheduling a bunch of appointments on short notice," I replied archly.

His slow grin had me clenching my thighs together to quell the ache building there. I hoped like hell no one noticed my blush. Hot as my cheeks were, I had no doubt I was flushed pink.

"I see. Well, far as I can tell, I'm all caught up."

"Did you take a look at the office?" I asked.

"Darlin', I was in the office all damn day."

"Not the exam rooms, the other office," I clarified.

His answering chuckle sent butterflies in flight in my belly. "I didn't even bother to look. As far as I'm concerned, that's your territory now. I told you we needed help, and I meant it. Do your worst, but preferably your best."

Somewhere during the course of those few sentences, I noticed his thigh pressing against mine. My sex clenched, and I felt a sheen of perspiration bloom across the surface of my skin. We were sitting here, surrounded by people, yet it felt as if the world had narrowed to this tiny space around us.

Sweet Jesus, I wanted Jackson. I would hold the memory of last night close in my heart. Because I finally had a good memory to replace too many bad ones. Last night had been so hot, I was fairly certain perhaps it burned away the bad ones. I wouldn't mind a few more to toss on that fire.

"Saw you working with Mischief earlier today. He likes you," Jackson commented in between bites.

I took a sip of wine and shrugged, unable to keep from smiling. "I like him too. He's a spunky little guy. He has no idea he's smaller than all the other horses."

"Oh, hell no. Mischief is living proof it's all about attitude. You let me know if you need help with him."

Glancing to the side, I collided with Jackson's blistering gaze again. It was a shock to my system all on its own.

"Of course. If you don't…" I began, pausing when he shook his head.

"I'm not worried about what you do with him, Shay. But I know it's been a few years since you worked with horses. That's all."

That far-too-familiar sense of insecurity and doubt had immediately begun to invade me. At his reassurance, it faded quickly. "Okay. Thanks."

He took a bite of his food and replied to something Wade said from across the table. I returned my focus to my own meal, studiously keeping my eyes away from Jackson.

When I looked up, I noticed Dani looking between Jackson and me. She was shameless and simply winked when I caught her staring at us. I shook my head. She looked away again when one of the guys teased her about something. Although I was starting to settle in, I was definitely the newest one here and mostly an observer. I enjoyed watching the easy teasing banter when they were all together.

I finished my dinner and refilled my glass of wine, my eyes falling to Jackson's forearms as he speared a piece of beef with his fork and twirled his now empty beer bottle in his other hand. Apparently, I had a thing for forearms. Or so

I was noticing when it came to Jackson. I savored the subtle flex of his muscles, the dusting of hair on his burnished gold skin.

My gaze traveled to his hands. Oh sweet Jesus, his hands. They were strong, his fingers long, and there were a few scars scattered across the backs of his palms. I knew exactly how his touch felt on me and inside of me. There was nothing cultured about his hands. He worked too hard for that to be the case. Strong and rugged as he was, I knew he would never hurt anyone. Although he certainly had the strength to do so, should he so choose.

Out of nowhere, a flashback struck, like lightning flickering in the corner of my mind. Clint had been polished. He was fit, but the sleek kind of fitness that came with working out. No one would ever say his hands were rugged or tough. Just now, I remembered his hand curling around my upper arm during a function for his father's last political campaign. He'd been wearing a suit and tie, of course. His fingers had dug into my skin through the thin silk of my blouse. The next day, I had bruises there, along with one low on my ribs, where he'd driven his fist into my side later that night.

I hadn't realized I'd gone still and stiff until I felt Jackson's palm slide along my thigh. "You okay there?" he asked, his voice low, only for my ears.

I jerked my head, colliding with his gaze. My heartbeat was rocketing erratically in my chest, and I struggled to manage a breath. "Yeah, yeah, I'm fine."

His eyes narrowed, his gaze coasting over my face, but I didn't want to talk, certainly not now.

Although I was startled and rattled by that flashback, somehow Jackson's touch soothed me. His palm, warm and strong, stayed resting on my thigh for a few minutes. One of the guys said something to him, and he replied, while I focused on reminding myself I was here. Nowhere near Clint.

The hum of voices carried on around me and eventually, my heart slowed its pounding, and I felt mostly normal. Well, except for the fact I couldn't seem to be anything other than hot and bothered around Jackson. Even on the heels of that disconcerting and frightening moment, as soon as it passed, I became acutely aware of his touch.

Dani stood to start clearing the dishes, and I took the moment to rise from the table. I didn't want to leave Jackson's side, but it was a bit ridiculous. I couldn't just sit there at the table forever, for the sole purpose of savoring his warm, strong presence beside me.

A few minutes later, I was deep into rinsing plates and putting them in a large industrial dishwasher at the back of the kitchen. Dani leaned her hips against the stainless steel table beside me and glanced over. "You don't have to do that, you know."

"I like to help. You don't have to cook for us every night either," I added with a grin.

She laughed at that. "I love to cook."

I rinsed the last plate, sliding it into place before pushing the entire rack sideways on the track. "Should I start this?"

"Not now. It's not full yet. This way, I can throw in the stuff I use tomorrow morning for the guests. You heading into town with us?" she asked.

A few of the guys had already left, Jackson along with them. I wasn't particularly a fan of going out to bars, if only because it reminded me of too many nights with Clint. He loved to be out and be seen. Whether I went with him or not, he would go out and get drunk. When he returned home, he would knock me around if I said one thing wrong. Until the very end, even when he was drunk, he was smart about it. He managed to only strike places where the bruising wouldn't be seen—my arms, my sides, and my abdomen.

It was hard to explain just how disorienting it was once you were caught in an abusive cycle. One wrong word, one wrong look, and you never knew what would set the person off.

"No," I said with a forced smile, willfully ignoring the memories that rushed to the forefront, "I'll pass. I'm pretty tired."

"Suit yourself," Dani replied as she pushed her hips off the table. "See you tomorrow at lunch?"

"Of course."

I figured this also gave me a clean way to get to the house and hopefully fall asleep before Jackson and I were alone there. My body and mind were more than a little confused about the mess I'd gotten myself into. I had no regrets, but I needed to walk a fine line and keep myself sane.

I returned to the quiet house alone and went to sleep, willing my mind not to dwell on Jackson and my body not to restlessly long for him.

Chapter Eighteen

JACKSON

Leaning forward, I kept my eye on the ball in front of me, sliding my pool cue back and striking forward with soft precision. One ball clinked against another, sending my shot neatly into the corner pocket.

Glancing up, I met Wade's eye roll. "Dude, you always fucking win. I shouldn't play with you."

I winked as I stepped away from the table. "You don't have to play with me. I can kick somebody else's ass," I offered with a chuckle.

Wade muttered something under his breath and quickly racked the balls to start another game. It was getting late. At Lost Deer Bar, the only ones left out from the lodge were Wade, Dani, Dawson, and me. Dawson was busy flirting with a woman off to the side of our game.

"Well, hey there, Jackson," I heard a voice call from behind me.

Turning, I found Sherri Johnson approaching. Her dark hair was pulled into a ponytail high atop her head, glossy in the dim lights of the bar. Sherri was a relentless flirt, one I'd been dodging periodically for years now. Her brown eyes swept up and down my body, and she smiled slowly.

Objectively speaking, she was gorgeous. Her long legs were poured into a pair of fitted jeans with a tight top showing off her cleavage. She stopped in front of me, resting a hand on her hip. "Are you going to blow me off again?" she teased.

"Not interested, Sherri. Don't take it personally. Why don't you go bother Wade?"

She rolled her eyes. "Because he's secretly in love with Dani, and we all know it."

"Can't argue with that," I agreed, glancing over to see if Wade was within earshot. He wasn't, but it wasn't as if he hadn't heard people tease him about this before.

Sherri let out a good-natured sigh, nudging me on the shoulder as she passed by. "Well, I hope you find a girl who gets to you someday."

With that, she sauntered off. At her words, only one woman flashed through my thoughts—Shay. I'd been busy as all hell today, but tonight at dinner had been sheer torture sitting beside her. I'd all but fled as soon as I could. As it was, my cock was barely under control, even now.

I didn't know what the hell to do about Shay. Because, fuck me, but I wanted her. When I felt her tense up tonight, an overwhelming sense of protectiveness had rolled through me. I spent most of today, whenever I had a moment to think, alternating between replaying our night last night and considering the ways I could somehow beat the living shit out of her ex, even though he was locked up in jail.

With a mental shake, I turned when Wade said my name, relieved to focus on another game of pool. By the time I returned to the house, it was going on two in the morning. This was late for me. It wasn't common for me to stay out like this.

Even though I hadn't allowed myself to dwell on it, I knew precisely why I had. It was an insurance policy, a guarantee that Shay would be sound asleep, and I wouldn't be tempted to crawl into her bed and lose myself in her.

I walked through the soft, cool spring air after I parked my truck, taking a few deep breaths and stopping on the porch to listen to the sound of the crickets calling in the quiet night. After I let myself in the house, I slipped my shoes off by the door and hung my jacket. I walked up the stairs, avoiding the areas that would creak. I knew those stairs by heart because I grew up in this house.

With Shay's bedroom at an angle across from mine, I reflexively stopped in the hallway. Hell if I knew why. A distressed sound filtered through her door. Not quite a cry, but damn close.

I moved without thinking, turning the knob to the door and stepping into her dark room. The light from the hallway cast across her bed, and I could see her shifting restlessly as she cried out again.

Before I knew what I was doing, I was approaching her bed and easing my hips onto the mattress beside her. I settled my palm on her chest, only to realize her heart was pounding wildly and erratically. She was terrified.

She came awake with an abrupt lurch, her entire body going stiff as her eyes opened wide.

"Don't!" The word flew from her mouth as her eyes landed on me. At first, she didn't appear to recognize me.

"Shay, it's me. Jackson."

She gave her head a shake, falling back against the pillows again. Her heartbeat was still thumping hard and fast. She looked away, taking a deep, shuddering breath.

"Oh," she said softly, her voice ragged. "What are you doing here?"

When she turned her head back, and I saw the guarded look in her eyes in the dim light cast from the hallway, anger bolted through me. Not with her, but with the man who had done this to her.

"I heard you in the hallway. It sounded like you were having a nightmare."

I told myself I should take my hand away from her, that she was awake now and would probably be fine. But I couldn't make myself do any of that.

"Oh. I guess I was."

The sound of her swallow was audible in the quiet room. Her heartbeat gradually slowed under my palm as I sat there. I eased it away, sliding it down over her side to rest on the curve of her hip.

"You okay now?"

She nodded, lifting a hand to brush her tangled hair away from her cheek. Next thing I knew, I was standing and bundling her into my arms.

"Um, Jackson, what are you doing?" she murmured, her sleepy voice tugging on my heart.

"My bed is more comfortable," was all I could come up with in reply. Somehow, I had determined she shouldn't be sleeping alone.

There was nothing sexual about this. I just couldn't bring myself to leave her by herself, not after hearing her the way her body reacted to whatever hellish dream she'd been having.

She seemed slightly befuddled, but didn't resist. I could still feel tension humming in her body.

In a moment, we were in my bedroom where the moon fell through the windows, casting the room in a silvery glow. I eased her down on the bed, tucking the sheets over her. I stripped out of my jeans and T-shirt to climb in beside her, not really wanting to talk, or even think about what the hell I was doing.

I pulled her against me as I curled up behind her. She was still quiet, but I felt the tension slowly easing from her body. When her ice cold feet bumped into my calves, I laughed. "Jesus, Shay. You're freezing."

"I get cold whenever I have a nightmare," she mumbled.

My heart clenched again. I simply held her. I didn't fall asleep until she did, until the cadence of her breath was slow and steady, and her body relaxed against me.

Chapter Nineteen

JACKSON

I had no idea what time it was when I woke. Shay's bottom, her lush, sweet bottom, was pressed against my arousal. She was still sound asleep.

The light was thin, and I knew the sun hadn't crested the mountains yet. The moment my consciousness flickered awake, and I became aware of Shay's warm body relaxed beside me, my cock hardened even further. It said something about the state of my body that, even in sleep, I was intensely aroused by her.

When I carried her in here last night, I would've sworn on a stack of Bibles sex had nothing to do with my intentions. All I wanted was for her not to sleep alone after that nightmare.

Those intentions had gone up in smoke. In the wispy light of dawn, I wanted her with such ferocity, I honestly didn't know if my good intentions could help me out of this jam.

As if to prove my point, Shay moved in her sleep, shimmying a little closer, the slide of her curves over my cock leaving me to bite back a low groan.

She shifted slightly again, her breasts jostling slightly. My hand wasn't listening to my mind and moved to cup her breast in my palm, brushing my thumb back and forth across her tight little nipple.

I inhaled her scent on a breath, leaning closer to taste the soft, sweet skin on the side of her neck. Arching on an exhalation, her bottom pressed closer, right where my cock was nestled between the sweet cheeks of her ass.

I told myself I was teetering on the edge of climax simply because it had been too damn long since I'd had regular sex. I wasn't abstaining, not on purpose, but not much caught my attention of late.

Every woman came with strings attached, or so it seemed. Although, if that was my excuse, Shay came with more strings than anyone I could imagine. She was temptation incarnate and rife with complication upon complication. My best friend's little sister, one of my sister's best friends, my own fucking baggage, and hers. Yet, raw desire ran roughshod over common sense. When she sighed again, I wanted more. I wanted to feel her fly apart in my arms again.

I felt the exact moment when she came awake. It just so happened to be when I dropped a kiss in the little divot above her collarbone. She rolled slightly toward me.

"Jackson," she murmured, her voice velvety and softened with sleep.

"Mmm-hmm," was all I had to say as I continued tasting her, savoring her little gasps.

She tensed slightly, but relaxed, letting out a low moan as I continued my lazy exploration. I teased her nipples and slid my palm down over her belly, dipping through her curls into the slick, hot center of her.

She was drenched, so ready. I had completely forgotten all of my promises to myself to keep clear lines between us. All I wanted right now was to be buried deep inside of her and find the release insistently pounding inside of me, demanding action.

When I slipped a finger into her core, she let out a soft whimper, the sound like a whip striking against me. Goose bumps rose on her skin as my teeth grazed lightly on her neck.

I added another finger to join the first, stretching her channel gently. Her hips arched into my touch. She was so fucking responsive. All on her own, she was beautiful, sensual, and so damn tempting.

When she shifted her hips again, a whispered plea slipping from her lips, it was all I could do not to simply bury myself inside of her right then. Not yet.

She turned in my arms, her eyes opening in the silvery gray light. Her green gaze was bright and sleepy. I teased in her folds, savoring the arch of her hips into my touch and the silky wet clench of her channel.

Dipping my head, I brushed my lips across hers. She hesitated and then welcomed me in, our kiss slow, sleepy, and sensual. It felt as if we were suspended in time, in that magical hour before night turned to day and the world was quiet. With her skin silky soft and warm, and the silvery dawn making everything shimmer, need spun so tightly inside I could hardly hold myself in check.

Shay's hands got busy mapping my chest, sliding over my shoulders, stroking across my cock through my briefs. I could feel her smile against my lips when my cock pulsed under her touch, swelling harder.

Lifting my head just slightly, so that my lips were moving against hers when I spoke, I teased, "Think that's funny?" Then, I stroked my fingers, knuckle deep, into her slick, pulsing channel.

Her breath hissed through her teeth with a little moan. Everything was somehow rushed and sleepy at once. Lust tightened inside of me, the flames of it licking at me. Somehow, I got her T-shirt off and her panties out of the way. She made quick work of my briefs, shoving them down with a hand and then pushing them off my ankles with her feet.

Then, we were skin to skin. She teased me, her hands stroking my cock, swiping the pre-cum off with her thumb and sucking it into her mouth.

Somewhere along the way, she took control. Sitting astride me and looking down, her hair was a wild, tangled mess around her shoulders. Her eyes were dark and teasing as she looked at me and then shimmied down, dropping hot little kisses across my chest and abdomen before swirling her tongue around the tip of my cock.

Her name came out in a low growl as I squeezed my eyes shut. "Jesus, Shay," I bit out as she dragged her tongue from the base of my cock to the tip, again swirling around the thick head.

Dragging my eyes open, I looked down to see her hair shielding her cheeks and her sly gaze catching mine when I murmured her name again. She kept her eyes on me as she sucked me fully into her mouth, the warm suction almost drawing my release from me. Scrambling inside, I shackled my control.

She worked me with her mouth, sucking, licking, and stroking in her wet grip. Heat flashed through me, tightening in my balls, my hand gripping her hair tightly as I clung to my control. As good as this felt—pure heaven and torture—I wanted to be inside of her when I let go. With a rough groan, I murmured, "Shay."

"Hmmm?" she hummed around my cock.

"Come here." I tugged on her hair lightly, and blessedly, she rose up. Her nipples were tight and pink, and I needed to taste her.

Leaning up, I caught a nipple with my mouth, swirling my tongue around it. I smiled against her skin in satisfaction when she cried out, gripping my hair as I shifted my attention to the other nipple.

I wasn't thinking. Nothing but lust drove me. She rocked

her hips back and forth over my cock. Resting against the pillows piled against the headboard, I looked at her, brushing her hair away from her face as she rose and started to slide down over me.

Abruptly, I realized I didn't have a condom on. I grabbed her hip tightly, muttering quickly, "Wait."

My tone came out sharp, because I was pushed to the edge of my restraint. Her eyes widened and she stiffened. In a flash, she was moving to scramble away, and I realized I had startled her.

"Hey," I said, catching her hand. She froze where she was, at an angle across my hips. "I just need to get a condom."

The tight and frozen look in her eyes faded. She didn't move, so I did, sliding my palm down her side, pausing to cup her breast. Part of me was tempted to say we should stop, but I sensed that would make this much worse in the moment. So I leaned forward, swirling my tongue around her nipple before easing her to her side and stretching out beside her.

We needed to slow this down. "Your turn," I told her.

Chapter Twenty

SHAY

"Your turn."

When I looked at Jackson, his dark brown hair mussed and his heated gaze lifting to meet mine, it felt as if sparks scattered through me at the delicious tease of his lips coasting over my abdomen.

I felt exposed and split wide open, still spinning slightly from that moment where I froze. Somehow, I didn't know how, Jackson seemed to know if we had stopped then, it would've been devastating for me. His hands were everywhere, lightly cupping a breast, mapping the soft curve of my abdomen, and sliding up my thighs to push my knees apart.

Whatever I meant to say was lost in my low moan when two fingers stroked inside of me as he brought his mouth to me, licking into my core. I cried out, the pleasure so piercing, it almost hurt. He settled into a steady rhythm with his fingers as he licked through my folds, his tongue teasing over my clit.

He proceeded to make me lose my mind. Everything blurred, all of my focus narrowing to the feel of his fingers and his mouth working over the most vulnerable part of me. As exposed as I felt, I couldn't stop the sensation spinning me into a wild storm of need, desire, and pulsing intimacy catching me in its center.

My release rushed over me when he swirled his tongue around my clit, giving it the slightest bit of suction. I cried out roughly, gripping his hair in one hand and the sheets in the other, my entire body shuddering so deeply it felt as if my bones were liquid.

Then, he was rising up, his mouth and hands making another slow exploration of my body on the way back up. As his weight settled over me, he tensed slightly.

"Be right back. Condom," he murmured, his voice tight as he started to roll away.

"Don't worry about it. I'm on the pill." I didn't want him to go anywhere.

Jackson froze where he was half-rolled off me, and I held him in place with my legs.

"It's your call," he said, his voice low.

"I know. But it's just me. And it's you, so..."

"It's your call," he repeated, "not mine." He paused, the silence abruptly heavy. "I've never had sex without a condom."

"Never?"

He shook his head and shrugged. "No ma'am. You knew my dad. He was a blunt man. Gave me the lecture of a lifetime when I was old enough to have sex, and scared the bejesus out of me."

I almost smiled because I remembered his father, so straightforward and direct. I could imagine he went out of his way to make sure Jackson used protection.

"And you knew my mom. She was all about making sure I started birth control before I ever had sex. The pill's kind of a thing for me too. Clint didn't want me to take it, so..." The topic had suddenly gotten serious, and Jackson's eyes narrowed.

"Sometime, you're gonna tell me a little bit more about what happened." His voice was low, his tone laced with anger.

Emotion slammed into me. I didn't want this moment to be tangled up with my past. "It's over. Forget about it."

Jackson was quiet, his eyes on mine, the blue even brighter in the wispy light of dawn. A sliver of sun crested above the horizon, a narrow ray angling through the window to the wall across from the bed.

"Okay," Jackson finally said, dipping his head and pressing hot, damp kisses along my shoulder and up the side of my neck. The soft touches set my nerves alight, sensation tingling all over.

Then, his weight was settling over me again, his cock sliding through my slick folds. One of his hands curled around mine where it rested on the pillow beside my head, his grip strong and sure. On an exhalation, he sheathed himself inside of me, filling me and stretching me in a slow surge.

He held still once he was buried within me, but my body was restless, my hips bucking into him. He muttered my name with a rough growl before drawing back and sinking in deeply. The angle was such that the pressure was just above my clit, teasing and sending piercing streaks of pleasure through me. It was already swollen, over-sensitized from the madness he wrought with his lips and tongue.

A few more slow thrusts, and I was already flying apart inside, the pressure spinning loose and scattering like hot sparks. I cried his name, my pussy throbbing and clenching around his cock. His release filled me in a surge of heat as he went taut over me, my name a muffled cry.

He fell against me, but shifted quickly, rolling us over in the bed so I was lying on top of him again. I held still, my heart thudding hard and fast inside my body as I listened to the answering beat of his own against my ear.

———

Later that morning, I groomed Mischief with a soft brush after we spent a good half an hour together in the paddock with a lunging lead. Although he was spirited, he settled quickly once he adjusted to something new. He'd stopped constantly biting at the saddle pad on his back and had decreased his chewing on the rubber snaffle bit.

I was anxious to start riding him, but I knew we needed to move slowly. He liked being groomed. It was clear he'd be happy to have someone pay attention to him all the time. His wild edge was definitely there, but he was so affectionate by nature that it helped. When it came to training, that was a major plus.

He turned his head, expectantly looking for one of the molasses grain treats I'd gotten in the habit of giving him after we finished grooming. I fished one out of my pocket and handed it over, rubbing his forehead as he chewed it.

"You ready to go see your friends?" I asked conversationally. Ever since I was a little girl, I had talked to animals as if they were people. It was a habit I couldn't seem to break. As I turned, a shadow caught the corner of my eye, and I flinched, freezing in place.

Yet again, a small trigger sent me spinning into a brief flashback. That night—the worst night of them all, when Clint raped me—I had been at home, standing at the end of the hallway in our condominium. I usually avoided Clint as best I could. I remembered seeing his shadow flickering in the corner of my vision and sensing his anger from a distance. Perhaps it was because I was so attuned to it, but somehow, I had known he was simmering with rage that night.

"Hey, Shay," Wade called as he rounded the corner of the aisle between the stalls.

I took a deep breath, willing my pulse to slow down.

"Hey, Wade," Jackson's voice called from right behind him.

It was only then I realized if I hadn't been temporarily frozen in fear, I likely would've heard Jackson's footsteps on the stairs from the vet offices above.

Wade glanced over his shoulder, grinning as Jackson followed him into the aisle. Jackson's eyes landed on mine. His gaze was assessing, coasting over me. He didn't say anything, but even from a good twenty feet away, I could sense he picked up on my brief moment of distress.

I looked away, focusing my attention on Mischief. I didn't have to worry about him or my reactions. He was easy. I stroked my palm down the side of his neck and unclipped the lead where he was hooked up for grooming.

"I was just about to take him outside," I said as I turned, walking toward where Jackson and Wade were standing. Wade had hooked his elbow over the edge of an empty stall, while Jackson leaned against the wall at an angle, idly kicking against the dirt floor with the heel of his boot.

Wade grinned as I passed by him with Mischief. Jackson didn't say anything, his eyes tracking me intently.

It had taken me most of the morning to pull myself together after the way I woke up with him. I was still crystal clear about where things stood with us. I had no expectations. The problem was my heart was making a bit of a racket about it. I was worried I might start to want something other than nothing when it came to Jackson.

Slightly rattled and shaken from my brief flashback, I kept my hand on Mischief's neck, taking comfort from his presence, as we walked through the archway and gate into the small paddock that led into the larger pasture. Slipping his halter off, I scrubbed behind his ears, a favorite spot for him. He leaned his head into my chest and made a rumbling sound in his throat, the pony equivalent of a purr.

"Go have fun with your friends," I said. As soon as I opened the gate, he trotted through, his tail high and his ears forward. His coat gleamed under the sun. I knew my grooming was a waste of time because he loved to roll in the dirt, but that didn't change the fact I enjoyed it. It was as much for me as it was for him.

Returning to the barn, I found Jackson and Wade chatting about supplies. I headed upstairs to the office after I quickly returned Mischief's halter and lead to the tack room. I practically ran out of there like a scalded cat. My encounter with Jackson in there had seared itself in my memory. I couldn't set foot inside without a vivid recollection of the feel of his mouth working over mine and his fingers sliding into my wet core.

Chapter Twenty-One

SHAY

The office was starting to feel a little bit like mine, although I'd never had my own office, so I didn't know how it was supposed to feel. Until after things were over with Clint, I hadn't realized the depth of the effect his isolation had on my life.

When I first became involved with Clint, I hadn't seen the darkness hiding under Clint's polished surface. My life gradually narrowed to college classes and the job I had waiting tables for extra spending money. Clint had wanted me to change my hours, even though the tips were better at night. I went along with it because I didn't care to argue.

That was only the beginning of how limited my life became. By the end, just about everything outside of Clint had been whittled away.

I shook those thoughts away. The one thing he hadn't tried to steal from me was my education. It wouldn't have been helpful for his reputation to be connected to a woman who didn't have a good college degree. I had graduated summa cum laude with a degree in Computer Science.

I'd yet to have a chance to use my degree, although I

figured it might come in handy for this job if I could do some work with the website. Beyond that, I loved organizing things, and there was more than enough for me to organize when it came to the office and administrative tasks. Jackson hadn't been lying when he said this area of the business had been neglected.

I'd taken the framework Dani created for the lodge reservations and applied it here for the vet clinic scheduling. That had been the easy part. The billing, the supply ordering, and all the rest were a bit of a train wreck.

I settled into work quietly. Fortunately, I had enough to focus on that I couldn't really dwell on Jackson. Another hour or so later, I recalled my promise to Dani that I would help with some cooking prep. The lodge occasionally hosted events for locals who reserved the restaurant. Although she had temporary staff to use, she told me she wanted the company.

I saved my work in the computer and made sure everything was put away. With it being spring in western North Carolina, evenings were getting warmer but they were still cool once the sun slipped behind the mountains. I snagged a lightweight windbreaker off the hook on the back of the door and headed over. When I stepped out of the office, I could hear Jackson's voice coming down the hallway from one of the vet examination rooms.

"So, you think he's okay?" a female voice asked, a coquettish lilt to it.

I paused in the doorway in the office, hating the fact that I wanted to listen.

"He's doing just fine," Jackson replied, his tone even and low and so damn sexy. I'd never been turned on by a man's voice before, but Jackson's struck a chord deep inside of me.

"Thank you so much, Jackson," the woman said.

I heard the sound of running water and presumed he was rinsing his hands in the sink beside the examination table. "Anytime. He's not due in for another six months, given how well he's handled his recovery from his hip surgery. So, just give the office a call to schedule."

"Oh, you're not scheduling your own appointments anymore?"

"Oh no. I handed that off. Shay Martin is our office manager now and handles all that."

A little buzz of joy spun through me at how officially he described my role. It seemed small, but it was monumental for me.

"Shay Martin? She was in the news, right?"

The moment the woman said my name, I knew she knew who I was. Anxiety tightened in my chest. Even though this wasn't my hometown, this was a small area. When Clint got arrested for his assault against me, and then within weeks for his DUI after the accident that killed two people, his name was splashed in the papers all over North Carolina. Seeing as his father was a long-time state politician, and Clint and I were dating, my name had been in the news as well.

I heard Jackson moving because I recognized the tread of his footsteps. That was how bad I had it.

"Yes, Shay Martin. Do you know her?" he asked.

"Well, it's hard not to know her. She was all over the news with everything that happened with Clint Glover. If you ask me, I still think it's up for debate how she fabricated those assault charges," the woman said primly.

I felt sick and suddenly weary. I had heard this line of thinking far too much.

There was a moment of dead silence. "Shay works here now. She's an old friend. I can't believe you would assume it's *any* woman's responsibility when someone beats the hell out of her. This wasn't a 'he said, she said' situation," he said flatly.

Jackson's voice was low and dangerous. I knew he was furious. I abruptly moved back into the office, out of sight, when I heard them step into the hallway.

"Oh, I didn't mean any harm. You know, just all speculation and so many rumors. It's hard to know what to believe," the woman said dismissively.

My line of sight offered a view of her hand, reaching out to curl around his upper arm. Although it wasn't blatant, the vibe she gave off was flirtatious.

I took a deep breath and let it out slowly.

Jackson didn't reply. "Right that way to the parking lot," he said, his tone curt. It was clear as day he wanted her gone.

"Of course. I'll call to schedule."

I heard her footsteps moving in the direction of the door to the parking lot. Her dog's claws clicked on the vinyl tile as they moved away.

I suddenly felt exhausted. In the aftermath of Clint's arrest, I had endured weeks of media scrutiny. We were living in Chapel Hill at the time, one town over from Raleigh, the state capital, where Clint's father reigned supreme. Reporters had camped out to snap pictures of me when I came and went from the condominium. Speculation ran rampant about what had led to him chasing me out of our condo and throwing me against the pavement.

Whether it was luck, fate, or my personal guardian angel, a witness who saw the start of the assault took photographs and caught some of it on video on their smartphone. Without that, Clint probably never would've been charged. Even then, I was still quite convinced he was only in jail now because of the DUI and the deadly accident.

I hoped and prayed Jackson thought I had left. I had no easy way out of here right now. I had left the office door open. If I closed it now, it would be obvious I was here. I simply leaned against the wall and breathed quietly.

I felt his presence before I saw him. "So, when she calls to schedule, do *not* give her an appointment," he said from the doorway.

I looked over. I didn't know how to read his expression. It was controlled, and I could see the lines of tension in his shoulders.

"You don't need to lose clients on account of me."

"Shay, whether you're here or not, I'm not gonna listen to bullshit rumors about you." He stepped into the office. I had turned off the light, leaving the room cast in the smudgy light of dusk. The hallway light angled across his face as he stepped in front of me, leaning his hands on the wall on either side of me. "You hear me?" he asked, his voice low but gentle.

I couldn't speak through the emotion tightening in my throat, so I simply nodded. My hands were balled into fists in my pockets.

Jackson appeared to be considering something, and then he dipped his head, quickly pressing a kiss to my lips. It was brief, but hot, sending a zing of electricity straight through my system.

"Dani tells me she rounded you up to help with dinner tonight," he said as he stepped back. All I could do was nod again. "I'll walk over with you."

That's how we ended up walking together over the slight rise through the trees, his presence strong and steady beside me.

Chapter Twenty-Two

JACKSON

I held tight to the rope as I rappelled down. "I'm there," I called up to Dawson in the darkness.

"Got a hold on you," Dawson called down in reply.

It was dark and raining. After Shay and I walked over for dinner at the lodge, the clouds hanging low on the horizon all afternoon had let loose the rain. Dawson and I were on call for Stolen Hearts Valley Emergency Response, and a call came in just as dinner was winding down.

While everyone else was planning to relax with a few drinks after dinner, we grabbed our gear and took off. A car leaving a nearby local bar had driven off the side of a cliff on one of the sharp turns along one of the many winding roads through the Blue Ridge Mountains.

Although the eastern mountains had lower elevation and held you close in the embrace of their hills and valleys, they tempted people to make reckless decisions. With their less stark and forbidding presence in relation to the mountains out west, people could be tricked into thinking they weren't dangerous. Yet, we had roads winding in the craziest places, deep in the mountains.

When the weather was bad, or when people were stupid, or perhaps a little drunk—which was my guess, seeing as this car had left a bar—sometimes bad accidents happened. I was familiar with this road, so even though it was dark, I had a sense of what we were dealing with. The car in question had come to a stop just below a tangle of trees where the steep cliff face shifted into more sloping terrain.

I loosened the excess rope on my end so I could slide down a little further. Cool spring rain pelted my face. Once I got my footing amongst the trees, I carefully looked around to see what we were dealing with. I was calm inside, although there was always a bit of adrenaline.

The car was cradled at an angle on its side in a nest of kudzu vines in the trees. The driver was unconscious when I peeked through the broken window. The single passenger on the far side was conscious, but bleeding. I could see the trickle of blood running down her hairline and cuts along her arm.

"How ya doing?" I called over.

The woman rolled her head to the side, the rain falling through the driver's side window and streaking the blood on her face. "Um, okay," she said, her voice reedy.

She was pinned in the car in such a way I knew this rescue wasn't going to be easy. "Okay," I said calmly, as I reached through and rested my fingers against the driver's neck, relieved to feel a steady pulse.

I spoke into my radio. "They're both alive, but we're going to need several of us down here to deal with this."

"Gotcha," Dawson replied.

"The passenger is conscious, and the driver is unconscious, but he's got a pulse."

"What do we need?" Dawson asked in return.

"I can't clarify the extent of their injuries at this time. We might need to stretcher them out, but I'm not sure. We need at least two more down here to start."

I figured that would give me enough for us to assess if we

needed stretchers or not. Dawson replied in assent. While I waited for more support, I proceeded to investigate what we were dealing with, the best I could under the cramped circumstances.

The next few hours passed in a blur. I handled it as well as could be expected. In these situations, I usually went down first. I was the lead on our team and the most experienced climber in the crew. When I first returned from the war, I had my doubts about returning to this work, but it was the only thing that kept me sane, in a strange way.

In the darkness and rain, I only had one flashback, and I beat it back quickly. It wasn't the rain that triggered it, nor the darkness, although that might have had a hand in it. Rather, it was when the driver became conscious while I was waiting for two others from my team to rappel down.

The man had groaned and asked in a disoriented voice, "What the fuck?"

The night I'd been with my team doing a sweep of an apartment complex to find a target, one of my closest friends had gotten blown to smithereens by an IED. He too had been unconscious for a few minutes, and asked that very question when he came awake briefly.

In the darkness, by that car, my chest tightened painfully. Grief could come spinning sideways like a knife flying through the sky sometimes. It sliced at you, a sharp, burning reminder of what was lost.

Hours later, I leaned against Nick Hudson's desk and ran my hands through my hair with a sigh. Nick was the administrative supervisor for emergency operations for Stolen Hearts Valley. "Damn lucky they were. That's all I got to say," I said.

Nick's silver hair glinted under the fluorescent lights as he nodded slowly. "Damn straight. They blew right through the guardrail. I keep telling the town they need to reinforce those. Some of those side roads are just too dicey."

"Based on the estimated speed, I don't know that any guard rail would've kept them off that cliff," I commented.

He cocked his head to the side and nodded. "True. You get your ass out of here and get some rest, okay?"

I nodded in return before pushing my hips away from his desk and heading out into the darkness. The rain had slowed to a drizzle. I was soaked through, but I wanted to get home for my shower.

Driving home, there was a tug, like a little string on my heart. Shay was home, and my heart knew it.

I knew, I fucking knew, I shouldn't have slept with her through to the morning. I shouldn't have kissed her tonight before we left the office. Shoulda, coulda, woulda. It didn't really matter what I should've done. Because I hadn't listened to a lick of common sense.

All I'd known was I didn't like the sound of Shay having a nightmare. I'd been downright furious at that bullshit comment that woman made after her appointment this afternoon. I mentally corrected myself. It was yesterday afternoon now, seeing as it was well past midnight.

It wasn't that I hadn't known Shay's ex had been splashed across the papers when everything went down. Hell, his family was way too high-profile to avoid it. Yet, it was fucking bullshit for anybody to question what happened. Remy had been worried as hell about Shay facing that media firestorm. He came home for a visit, and even considered moving back, because he was so worried. When it had all originally gone to hell for Shay, according to Remy, she wanted to see out the lease at the condo because the rent was already paid for the year.

Tonight should have reminded me why I couldn't be the kind of man she needed. Under the wrong circumstances, someone saying "what the fuck" left me breathless for a minute, my heart beating so hard it almost made me sick.

But god fucking dammit, Shay had gotten to me.

I cut the lights on my truck once I turned down the

drive to the house. I knew this road blind and in the dark. Seeing as it was going on two in the morning, I figured she must be asleep, and I didn't want the headlights to wake her. Keeping my tread light, I walked up the stairs, pausing by her door, relieved to hear absolutely nothing.

Weary and chilled from working in the rain for hours, I took a hot shower, staying in there long enough for the heat to wash the chill away. Although summer would be here soon enough and the nights would be warm, a rainy spring evening in the Blue Ridge Mountains was enough to make you cold to the bone.

I climbed into my bed, more aware than I wanted to be of the subtle pull to have Shay here beside me. Oh, there was lust wrapped up in it, the temptation to lose myself in the wild attraction between us. Yet, there was also a yearning for more of the way I felt when I was with her. Connected, linked by invisible threads that had more strength than I could've ever suspected.

Chapter Twenty-Three

JACKSON

Sleep wasn't claiming me, not in the hours of the dark morning. My thoughts did funny things when I had flashbacks. That one had been so brief, yet quite powerful. If the mind were a room, it was like the flashbacks came in and knocked everything out of order. You never knew where anything was going to land. My mind was spinning on its wheels. One wheel was filled with thoughts of Shay and my frustration with what I had walked into with her. The other wheel spun with regret, the same record playing again and again and again.

There was what I knew intellectually—war sometimes made people die. Sometimes those were people who mattered deeply, and sometimes you carried scars carved from the mixed feelings about a war tearing up another world. Then, there was the emotional piece.

Mike had been one of my closest friends. We'd worked our way up together in the Marines and shared many missions when we were together in Special Ops. When you work at that elite level, trust is beyond critical. His death had left deep scars of grief.

Rolling onto my side and adjusting the pillow, I looked at the clock. Somehow a full hour had passed since I climbed in bed. It was now three a.m. I toyed with getting up. There were always animals to feed, or a list a mile long of things to do.

Blessedly, sleep took hold with Shay dancing through my dreams. I woke with a start, the sun shining brightly and falling in a wide path across my bed.

I woke from a dream about Shay. It started out good—because she was nothing but good to me—but it had taken a tangled turn. Somehow, my dream state had manufactured a recollection of her ex beating her in that parking lot.

It wasn't as if that recollection came from nothing. Although I certainly hadn't been there—hell, I was nowhere near her at the time—pictures had been splashed all over the news. Not many, but enough. A blurry photo from a distance of her ex shoving her, the crime scene tape, and blood on the pavement. Not much, but just enough to make me crazy.

I was tense all over and my heart was pounding so hard, the beat vibrated through my entire body. Anger and sadness twined like vines together inside. I hated what she had gone through. I wished I could personally take down her ex. Kicking the covers back, I stood and walked into the bathroom, staring at myself in the mirror.

My hair stood up in spiked tufts and my eyes were bleary. I laughed humorlessly. I suppose it was fucking lucky that her ex was locked up. I couldn't trust what I would do if he wasn't. I knew Remy felt exactly the same way.

The moment I thought about Remy, a pang of guilt stabbed at me. Remy would most definitely have an opinion about Shay and me. I sure as hell had opinions about who Ash got involved with. The guilt was even stronger because I knew what Shay went through, and because I knew this thing between us could never be more than it was. No matter how much I wanted more.

Although my flashbacks had lessened, I still didn't have

faith I could be the kind of man any woman deserved, much less Shay. With a muttered curse, I turned away from the mirror and climbed into the shower. At this point, it wasn't to get clean, seeing as my last shower had only been hours earlier. It was just a way to wake myself up.

Making my way downstairs, I was relieved I didn't have any vet appointments today. I had enough else going on. In my state, I didn't need to be dealing with too many people. The animals were no trouble. It was always the people.

When I walked into the kitchen, I found a sticky note on the counter in front of the coffee maker.

Coffee is ready to go. Just hit start. I didn't know what time you'd be up. There're also scrambled eggs and sausage ready. I left a plate in the refrigerator. All you need to do is heat it up.

Shay

Out of nowhere, a bolt of grief hit me. Enough to make me grit my teeth. Grief for what I had lost.

Shay was just, well, she was just sweet. Hell, she was a lot more than sweet. She was hot as fucking hell when she was skin to skin with me.

Things like this—having coffee ready for me, making breakfast, simply caring about my welfare—these were all things I told myself I couldn't have. It was best if I kept my life circumscribed to friends who didn't expect too much, and animals. Although my father couldn't have known it when he formalized the rescue program at the farm, it was a fitting endeavor for me after I returned from the war.

I wasn't looking to be rescued. I certainly didn't need it, but as different animals passed through here, each carrying a complicated past, I learned from each one. I threw myself into the challenge of getting the dogs who hid in corners and wouldn't look at anyone to eventually relax and make eye contact. Give me a dog with anxiety-based aggression due to some asshole owner beating the shit out of it, and I would work for as long it took to show the dog that not all humans would hurt him. Give me a horse who had been starved and left for nothing and was skittish around people, and I would give her the same patience.

None of that was hard. Nothing I had to work for. And it filled me up in a way nothing else would. But when it came to people, especially people who deserved more than I could give, well, I was at a loss.

———

Later on that afternoon, I heard from one of the guys when they were returning from a guided hike that a section of fencing at the far end of the pasture had been broken through. We had plenty of land, and I preferred to let the horses roam, so the pasture went beyond the open field into the foothills of the mountains. Every so often, a horse broke through.

I was willing to bet money it was Mischief living up to his name. Again. I debated hopping on my steady old gelding, Ranger, to ride out and investigate, but decided against it. Mischief tended to view any other horse as a reason to play.

I got distracted by a few other things before I had time to go take a look. When I headed into the trees and up the incline into the foothills, I looked up when I heard a voice.

Shay was ahead of me on the trail. This wasn't technically a hiking trail, per se, but it was a path the horses frequently used, so it was well worn. Mischief walked along Shay's side, his head low as she rubbed his ears, crooning softly to him.

She hadn't seen me yet, so I waited until they got closer. "Hey there," I finally said.

Mischief's ears perked up as he lifted his head. Shay followed his gaze, her eyes wide. She looked startled and frozen stiff, but masked her reaction quickly. "Oh, Jackson. I told Dawson I was going to look for Mischief. Dawson said to tell you he'd repair the fence this evening. Since

Mischief's pretty comfortable with me, I figured I could catch him."

"Dawson must've gotten tied up and forgot to let me know. No worries. It just saves me the time trying to round him up."

I reached into my pocket, pulling out one of his preferred grain treats. When I held my palm out flat, Mischief nibbled the treat up, rubbing his forehead against Shay's shoulder when he was done. I turned, falling into step beside Shay. She gave off a jittery and restless energy. I had to bite my damn tongue to keep from asking if she was okay.

We hadn't had much of a chance to talk since last night after that woman made her fucked up comment about Shay. Dinner was a crowded affair as usual, and then I'd been called out.

Now didn't seem to be the time to bring that up. I knew I had startled Shay. Startling her was not a good thing, and I didn't like to think about why.

"Thanks for the coffee and breakfast this morning," I said, my eyes on the trail ahead of us.

"Of course. I knew you didn't have appointments today, and Dani told me you were out until almost two in the morning. I figured you could use the coffee. Plus, you know me, I can't help myself, so I had to make some breakfast."

Shay loved to cook. Back when we were all younger and I used to spend the night with Remy, she was always in the kitchen with her mother.

"Of course you did," I told her with a chuckle.

We walked the rest the way in silence, aside from the occasional snort from Mischief. I almost reached out and caught her hand in mine, realizing what I was about to do in the nick of time. *Danger, danger*.

As much as I wanted to touch her, I had to keep things on an even keel. When we reached the barn, Shay led Mischief into his stall, quickly brushing him down. I was relieved to be distracted with chores since it was feeding time. Without even needing to discuss it, we both got to work. Between the rescues and the horses, it took roughly an hour.

I was in the tack room later, hanging up a few loose leads. This room also served as storage. It was basically a catchall for odds and ends. The door opened, the spring hinge squeaking slightly, and I glanced back to see Shay entering. She had a few halters looped over her shoulder and a bag of the treats for the dogs in her hand.

She glanced up, her cheeks flushing slightly when she saw me. "I think that's about it," she commented as she turned away to hang up the halters. "Gloria keeps sneaking food from one of the dogs."

I grinned. "She *is* a pig, although they don't quite deserve the connotation."

Shay smiled in return, and I was relieved to see her earlier tension appeared to have dissipated. Without thinking, I closed the distance between us. She was standing by the door, with one hand resting on an empty saddle rack.

By the time I noticed my body was following the magnetic pull to her, I was standing right in front of her. The light was dim in here, with nothing but the lingering rays of the setting sun angling through the windows at the back.

The rose gold-tinged light shimmered in her hair. It had fallen loose from its ponytail since we parted ways to take care of the evening chores and was in a tousle around her shoulders. Her tongue darted out, moistening her lips.

Sometime in the last few moments, my cock had begun to swell. The second her scent drifted to me, blood shot to my groin, and I felt the press of my zipper.

Shay was so fucking beautiful. I didn't know what to make of the depth of my response to her. I'd known her for what felt like forever. The memories of those halcyon days of childhood were like faded sepia photographs.

Remy and I were rough-and-tumble boys, and Shay and

Ash were always running along behind us back then, annoying the hell out of us. When I was old enough to notice her as a woman, I had more discipline about her. Perhaps it was because not only did I have Remy to contend with, but the shared disapproval of our parents if I made a move on my best friend's little sister. By the time she was in high school and flat-out gorgeous as she filled out, I was in college. Fortunately, distance and only passing encounters kept me in check.

I went off to the military, and my life changed, everything else falling to the wayside. Meanwhile, Shay started dating Clint Glover with his high-profile political father. I recalled Remy complaining about him, thinking he was a jerk even before Remy knew how violent he was to Shay.

And now, here she was. In all of her glory, she was sexy as fucking hell—take my breath away and knock my knees out kind of sexy. I needed *all* of my discipline to keep myself in check. Yet, whenever I was close to her, my best intentions dissolved into smoke.

In the quiet of that small room, I couldn't resist kissing her. My hand slipped out, my thumb brushing over the wild beat of her pulse along the soft skin of her neck. Raw, fierce desire took hold.

The moment my lips met hers, an electric jolt hit my system. Shay tensed slightly, and then let out a soft sigh, her tongue darting out and slicking against mine. Seeing as I had no control over the lust ruling me, everything she did was like pouring gasoline on a fire.

Chapter Twenty-Four

SHAY

I was burning up inside, fire sparking in my veins. Jackson crowded against me, and my back bumped into the door behind me. I was relieved for the support. Otherwise, I would've simply melted.

I was messy and dirty after a long day. I smelled like dust and dirt, and probably carried the scent of every animal I'd encountered today.

Sexy definitely wasn't how I felt. That didn't seem to matter to Jackson. Once his lips met mine, I forgot everything. His kisses were something else. They made me crazy—masterful, slow, and teasing. His tongue tangled with mine before he drew back, dropping soft kisses at the corners of my mouth and catching my bottom lip in his before diving in again. My nipples were tight and achy, and I could feel his arousal pressing against my lower belly. My sex clenched, and my panties were wet.

I'd spent most of the day silently lecturing myself on how I needed to get a grip on this thing with Jackson. It was spiraling out of control. Yet, the moment he was near, I forgot everything. Desire took over, and common sense went running.

I was gasping and moaning when he broke free, his lips dusting hot kisses along the side of my neck. With soft little nips, the graze of his teeth, and the scrape of his stubble brushing against my skin, shivers raced through me.

"Fuck, Shay," he murmured as he cupped one of my breasts in his palm, his thumb brushing back and forth across my tight nipple. With a gasp, I arched into him, rocking my hips over his knee when he slid it between my thighs. "I need you."

The rough edge to his voice sent my belly spinning in flips, and I felt as if I were falling. All I managed was a muttered gasp in return. Suddenly, the sound of a voice out in the barn filtered through the door. I recognized Dawson's teasing laugh.

Jackson froze, his lips soft on my skin in the divot between my collarbones. He lifted his head slowly, his eyes intent on mine.

After a beat, his gaze shuttered. "I'm sorry, Shay," he murmured, stepping back quickly. "This is crazy."

He spun away, striding over to stare out the windows, his back to me and the lines of tension in his shoulders evident. A sense of anger came off of him. It confused me and frightened me. I had no way of understanding how to deal with anger from any man, much less in this situation.

I did the only thing I could. I opened the door and walked out. I schooled my expression to calm. I was an expert at that. Dawson had blessedly stopped in the aisle, leaning down to greet Squeaky, who was at his feet. I couldn't help but laugh because the sight was so incongruent.

Dawson, a total flirt and player, handsome as all get-out, almost on his knees in the dusty aisle, carrying on a conversation with a tiny pig.

Dawson looked up, flashing a roguish grin. "Well, hey there, Shay. How's it going?"

I was thankful for the dim lighting in the barn. The setting sun was cast through the windows in the back, dust motes glittering in the air.

"Hey, Dawson," I replied, clearing my throat when I heard how breathy my voice sounded. "It's going just fine. What brings you over this way?"

Although I hadn't been here that long, I'd already gained a sense of the rhythms around here. For this part of the farm, where the rescue and horse barns were, mostly Jackson and me were around. Dani or Wade would stop by occasionally for management questions, but that was about it. This was the first time I'd encountered Dawson over this way.

"I came to see you, of course," he teased as he straightened, just as Jackson stepped out of the tack room behind me.

Dawson flirted with basically everyone. I had absolutely no doubt he was teasing with me.

Although I had lost my touch with flirting ever since Clint, Dawson made it easy, if only because he was so indiscriminate and friendly. I was quite certain he would flirt with a wall, if given the opportunity.

I grinned and shook my head. "You're not here to see me, Dawson."

Dawson shrugged. "Okay, can't fault me for trying."

Jackson had reached my side, and I felt a subtle tension emanating from him. When I glanced his way, his eyes were narrowed in Dawson's direction. It wasn't as if he hadn't seen Dawson flirting with anyone and everyone—men, women, and animals alike. Yet, if I didn't know better, I would've sworn he might be a little jealous, or rather, territorial.

Dawson wasn't the least affected. He caught Jackson's eyes and winked. "Nah. I just came over because Dani told me to. Apparently, I was the only one without enough to do at the moment. Anyway, she thinks you added an extra reservation at the lodge without confirming with her, and now we've got a group of hikers here and nowhere to put them."

"Oh fuck," Jackson muttered, running a hand through his hair and sighing heavily. "I probably did. Last month, I made the mistake of answering the phone over there. Dani was out doing something—I think getting eggs from the chicken coop—and I jotted down their names. I swear to God, though," he said, looking between Dawson and me, "I told them it wasn't a sure thing."

Dawson grinned. "Good luck with that, my man. I'm about to head into town on a store run. Need anything? Because I got no solution. I'm just the messenger. And my cabin only sleeps one, so I'm no help. We do have that one empty cabin."

Jackson sighed again. "Grab a few six packs of beer while you're out. Just throw it on my tab."

"Want me to deliver a message back to Dani?" Dawson asked good-naturedly. "She can tell me off, but I won't take it personally because I got nothing to do with this."

Jackson barked a laugh. "I can deal with Dani."

"All right, catch you later." Dawson leaned down and blew a kiss at Squeaky before turning and strolling out of the barn.

Squeaky looked up, wiggling her nose before turning and following Dawson.

I looked at Jackson. "So what do we do when something like this happens?"

Jackson shrugged. "I remember exactly why I never, ever answer the phone over at the lodge. Hate to tell you, but it's a group of eight. We have two options. Tell them it was a mistake and offer them a few free nights later on. Or, you and I stay in that cabin, and they get the house. If we're going to do that, we need to get the place tidied up quick. Ash has guest linens, or at least that's what she calls them. We've done this before, so it's not exactly new."

I stared at Jackson, my stomach tumbling inside and my

heart thundering. I had seen the tiny cabin in question. Dani had shown it to me one afternoon, and said if I didn't want to stay at the farmhouse, I could move there. It was small, and there was a single queen bed in there.

"How many days?" My voice came out breathy again.

"Five."

I stood there, chewing the inside of my cheek. I knew Jackson was waiting for me to make this call.

"How bad is it if we send them away?"

"It's not horrible. They'll be pissed, and we'll lose some money. I mostly feel bad because they came from out of state, so that means I'll be scrambling to find somewhere else for them to stay."

I took a deep breath and squared my shoulders. "Well, then I guess we're staying in the cabin." I turned and started walking out of the barn.

Jackson caught up to me in seconds. "You sure you don't mind?"

"It's not a big deal. It's five days. It's enough that you and Ash invited me to stay here. It's even more that you're paying me to work. I'm not going to screw up a reservation just because I'm here. I know that if it weren't for me, we wouldn't even be having this conversation."

Suddenly, emotion slammed into me. Just thinking about it reminded me of the last few years of my life. I was safe, I had a place to stay, and the ability to worry about minor things. For example, my inconvenient attraction to Jackson. It was a luxury in a way, the kind of thing that most people called a first world problem. I didn't think that was quite right. I wouldn't pretend like I knew what it was like to live in a war-torn country. But I knew what it was like to live in fear every day. I knew what it was like to not have anything of my own and not know where to turn. If it hadn't been for the grace of God and the blessings of our friends, I would be scrambling to get by right now.

The fact that safety and small worries were a gift had me

choked up. I walked swiftly across the gravel parking area between the barn and the house. When I reached the stairs at the house, I felt Jackson's hand curl over my shoulder.

"Shay." Jackson's voice was low.

I came to a stumbling stop on the top step. When I turned back, he was a step below me, so our faces were almost level.

"What?" I asked, the word coming out thick from the emotion caught in my throat.

"You okay?"

Jackson's eyes searched my face, and I suddenly felt exposed. I hated the sense of vulnerability I carried almost all the time. It was such a relief to be out from under Clint's grip, but I wasn't used to needing anyone.

Or rather, I wasn't accustomed to tolerating this feeling of not knowing if I could get by on my own. I carried a niggling sense of guilt around Ash too. She never said a word to me about it, but she was one of the friends I almost lost during my years with Clint. Not on purpose, but I let him isolate me from everyone. When it felt like everything turned against me, Ash had been there. Without hesitation. With no conditions, and with nothing but support.

Do not cry, do not cry, do not cry, I chanted silently, forcing myself to keep my eyes on Jackson's.

I nodded, but Jackson still didn't seem satisfied. "You don't look okay. What is it?"

It was incremental, but he moved a little closer, one hand resting on my hip. Oh geez. He needed to stop touching me. I craved it too much. Just that small point of contact, the heat of his palm sifting through my jeans, and it soothed me.

I took a shaky breath and let it out. "I'm okay. Really. Sometimes..." I lifted a hand in a shrug, stuffing it in my pocket after I let it fall. "It's been a hard year. It means a lot that you and Ash offered to let me stay. I don't want you to do anything different than what you would do if I wasn't here."

His gaze bored into me. "Shay, of course I want to ask if it's okay where we stay. If it were any of the other people here whose bedroom I was asking them to give up, I would ask their opinion. I'm not treating you any differently."

I held his gaze and nodded slowly. I knew he would do exactly that. "Okay." I started to turn and walk in the house. I was amped up and restless inside. Whenever the reality of my situation came into focus, I felt jumpy, wanting to shake off the sensations and how I felt inside.

After Clint was charged, the police had brought over a domestic violence support person to talk with me. She had very nicely referred me to a therapist. Although I hadn't really been up for it because I was swimming in layers and layers of shame, I went anyway because I felt so damn alone, and I needed someone to talk to.

I remembered her saying that this would happen. That my emotions might manifest physically, and I could look to my body for cues of times when I needed to take care of myself. I hadn't had the heart to tell her that I didn't know if I would ever learn how to do that.

I spun back around, my words flying out in a rush. "Don't go thinking I'm some kind of crazy basket case. I'm okay. I don't know what you thought when I spilled out all that stuff the other night, but I'm okay. Just treat me the way you would've before."

Jackson had crested the top stair and looked down at me, his blue eyes bright in the silvery light of dusk. "I may not know much, but I know damn well that what happens to us changes us. I don't think you're crazy. No more so than me," he said with a bitter laugh. "Let's get in the house and get things ready. As it is, I need to call Dani and tell her the plan."

On the one hand, I wanted to fling myself into his arms. And on the other, I somehow knew what I needed was to square my shoulders and carry on. So that's what I did.

In a flurry of activity, I got the four bedrooms upstairs

guest-ready while Jackson dealt with organizing the down-stairs. Conveniently, as Jackson had said, Ash had labeled one closet with instructions to prep the upstairs for guests. Over the years, in the old rambling farmhouse, different areas had been repurposed. Unlike newer homes, there wasn't an open floor plan, so it was simple to use the doors to close off areas to guests.

The downstairs section of the house was mostly closed off, except for the living room. Guests would have the run of the upstairs though. Within a half an hour, I walked out to see nothing more than a sliver of the orange ball of the sun above the horizon in the distance, orange and red bleeding into the darkness taking hold.

Jackson stood at the foot of the stairs. When he looked up, my breath hitched. In the soft glow of the light from the porch, his blue eyes were bright, his dark hair glinting. He wore his usual outfit—faded jeans that hugged his legs and a T-shirt. The only thing that appeared to change was the color. Today, he wore navy, which brought out the blue in his eyes.

"Were you waiting for me?" I asked.

I had packed enough clothes for the next five days and slung my duffel bag over my shoulder.

"Of course," he said simply.

My heart gave a hard thump, and I sternly ordered my body to behave. I needed to get this wild attraction to Jackson under control, sooner rather than later. The next five days were going to be a bit of a challenge.

I was relieved after we dropped our stuff off at the small cabin and headed over to the lodge. There, we were surrounded by the cluster of Jackson's friends that I was starting to feel were mine.

There was only one problem. Right before we walked in the back door to the employee area of the lodge, Jackson caught my elbow lightly.

"What?" I asked as I looked up at him.

Chapter Twenty-Five

JACKSON

Hours later, I walked through the soft spring darkness, the air scented with greenery gradually unfurling. I paused in the clearing before the cabin and hoped—hell, I fucking prayed —Shay was sound asleep. I'd made up some bullshit excuse for why I wasn't walking to the cabin with her after dinner. I figured the only way I could get through these nights and keep my hands off of her was if I got there after she was asleep. Leaning my head back, I looked up at the stars, bright in the darkness.

When I stepped into the cabin, the only light on was in the bathroom, cast at an angle through the back corner of the room. A quick glance at the bed, once my eyes adjusted to the dim room, indicated she was asleep. Relief washed through me, followed immediately by disappointment.

The problem was, I wanted Shay so much my cock was hard simply being in this room with her. But we both carried too much of our pasts with us. She needed a man who was rock solid. Not a man like me. I understood all too well what she was facing. Although what I had been through was quite different, I knew the triggers. I knew the feeling of being frozen, of feeling like you're an emotional landmine with the way you lugged your past along with you, wishing you could fling it away, trying and never quite succeeding.

With a silent sigh, I slipped off my boots and went into the bathroom to change. I usually slept naked, but tonight I slept under the covers with my briefs on and even a T-shirt. I might get hot, but I figured that would give me a little bit of armor.

The moment I tugged the covers up, she rolled over, sighing softly in her sleep and burrowing against my side, hitching a leg over mine. I didn't quite know what I had done to deserve this form of torture, but these next five nights were going to be fucking hell.

I could feel the soft give of her breast pressing on the side of my chest and her silky skin against my leg. I closed my eyes and started counting.

Shocking even myself, I actually fell asleep. Although, it was all for naught. I woke at some point later, in the darkness, with Shay's bottom pressed against my hard cock and her breast cupped in my palm. I was so fucking hard, I could've gone off at any second.

Suddenly, Shay turned in my arms. "Not fair," she said, her voice husky.

"What?" I murmured in reply, my own voice thick from sleep and desire.

"You keep saying this is crazy, and I keep trying to keep a little distance. Now, you've got your hands all over me and I'm all hot and bothered," she muttered, sounding somehow offended and sexy all at once.

I couldn't help but laugh, a little zing of joy spinning through me. Because this Shay—with a hint of sauciness and sarcasm—was the Shay I had known when she was younger. In my defense, I was half-asleep.

She rolled against me, one of her knees sliding over my thigh and brushing against my aching arousal. My breath hissed through my teeth. "Well, at least, you're in as bad a shape as me," she said with a giggle.

As my eyes adjusted to the darkness, her features came in to focus. There were two nightlights in this cabin, casting just enough of a glow that I could see the glint in her eyes and the gold sheen of her hair. "We need to talk about this," she added.

"Now?"

Shay nodded vigorously. "Yes."

Fuck me. She wanted to discuss *this* in the middle of the night in bed.

My mind told me one thing, which was to tell her there was nothing to talk about and we just couldn't do anything about this. My body, however, shouted over my mind.

"We don't need to talk, Shay, we need *this*."

Then, I threaded my hand in her hair, leaning up just enough to exert a subtle pressure to bring her mouth to mine. If she meant to resist, she didn't even try.

Her lips met mine in a blazing hot point of contact, a little moan escaping into our kiss. She shifted atop me, every glorious, soft, curvy inch of her. She was a bundle of warmth and lusciousness.

I groaned into her mouth, sliding my hand free of her hair and down her spine to cup her sweet ass. She meant business, drawing back, nipping at my bottom lip and then stringing kisses down my neck as she shoved my T-shirt up. "Why are you even bothering with this?"

Her hand slid up under my shirt, breaking our kiss long enough to yank it over my head. Any resistance was all in my head and an utter lie. The moment she put her lips to mine, I was lost in the tornado of fierce desire between us.

She trailed kisses down over my chest as I caught my hand in the thick fall of her hair. She wasted no time, shoving my briefs down and curling her palm around my cock. Her tongue swiped over the drop of pre-cum rolling down the underside of my cock, her mouth closing around me with warm, wet suction.

My head fell back into the pillows with a groan, a muttered curse, and her name. With her teasing fingers and mouth, she pushed me to the edge. I was clinging to my control, but I wanted to come inside of her. She was having none of it though. When I grabbed her hair and gave a tug, she giggled, a little hum around my cock. She drew me all the way in again, until the head bumped against the back of her throat. With the grip of her fist around the base of my cock, my release hit me swiftly, her name a rough cry in the quiet of the night.

She rose up slowly, and I dragged my eyes open. She had fallen asleep in a tank top that did next to nothing to hide the lush curves of her breasts. If I thought pouring my release into her mouth had slaked my need for her, I was mistaken. The moment her hips settled over mine and I felt the wet heat of her through the thin cotton of her panties, my cock thickened again.

I took a moment to simply look at her. With her lips puffy and swollen from the madness she had wrought with my cock, her cheeks flushed, her hair a tangled mess around her shoulders, and her nipples pressing tight against her tank top, she was so fucking sexy, she stole my breath and set my heart to thundering.

I slid my palms up under the hem of her tank top, letting it ride up along my wrists as I pushed it up. I groaned aloud when her breasts were exposed. I leaned up, catching a nipple in my mouth, licking and then giving a hard suck as I shoved the tank top over her head and flung it to the floor.

Her fingers speared my hair as she moaned and arched into my mouth. Two could play this game, and I set out to make her as crazy with need as possible. Drawing back, I blew lightly on her damp nipple, savoring the sound of my name, her voice husky and ragged with need. I teased the other nipple and dragged my fingers through the moisture left behind.

She was rocking her hips over my cock, which was hard to the point of pain all over again. I shifted up on the pillows and rolled her over, stretching out beside her. Still toying with her nipples, my palm slid down over the soft curve of her belly, feeling it ripple under my touch as her breath came in rough pants. I loved the sounds she made when she was aroused. Soft cries, little whimpers, my name interspersed among pleas. Here and there, I heard the sound of surprise and distantly wondered just how much she had missed out on before.

Mapping my way down her body, I curled my fingers over the elastic of her panties and dragged them down her legs. She assisted with a kick of her feet. Then, I was pushing her knees apart and burying my face between her thighs. The taste of her alone was an elixir, sending streaks of lust to spin inside the beat of a pounding need. She cried out when I buried my fingers in her slick, wet core.

Slow licks, followed by swirls of my tongue around her clit as I slowly fucked her with my fingers. I lifted my head to watch when she flew apart with a little suction on her clit.

She sighed when I kissed my way back up her body, my weight settling into the cradle of her hips. I brushed her tangled hair away from her face, watching as her eyes opened. She was soft against me, her nipples damp against my chest, and her body a welcoming haven.

In the past, I had a few semi-serious relationships, but nothing that tugged at my heart. Not the way Shay did. I couldn't even define what was happening between us. Perhaps it was because I'd known her for so long, perhaps it was the intensity of the elemental desire between us, or perhaps it was the intimacy that I didn't know how to explain, but which wound around us tightly, shimmering in the air, its own potent force.

My cock was nestled against her slick folds, and she

shifted her hips, restless. I gritted my teeth and tightened my fingers around one of her hands, which had somehow ended up in mine.

In the dark room, with nothing more than the nightlights casting a thin silver glow, I could see something flickering in her gaze. I didn't dare speak, not with my heart pounding so hard the beat echoed through my body.

As messy as the desire was between us, I could handle it. I didn't know how to handle this feeling, so I dipped my head and grazed my teeth along the side of her neck. I knew this was a hypersensitive spot for her. It never failed to send goose bumps prickling over her skin. She arched up against me, and my hips flexed back. It was a slow slide into her hot, clenching channel. I was halfway home when I realized I hadn't even considered a condom.

I froze, but she curled her legs around my hips, hers bucking into me. My body reacted instantly as I seated myself fully inside of her. I rose up slightly, opening my eyes. "I forgot a condom. I think..."

She shook her head wildly. "Didn't we already have this conversation? I'm on birth control, so I'm not worried about that. I got tested for everything under the sun after I found out what Clint had been up to. You don't need to worry about anything. Except for you, he's the only man I ever had sex with. I trust you."

My heart clenched like a fist inside my chest, an unfamiliar pain shooting through me. I wouldn't quite call it pain, more that I didn't know what the hell to do with the depth of emotion that was crashing over me, catching me in its undertow and pulling me under.

I was about to stop, but this had to be Shay's call, not mine. I worried she was reading too much into all of this.

Fool.

My brain countered quickly. *She's not reading too much into it. You're fucking scared.*

"But, Shay, this is..." I stopped when she shook her head sharply again.

"Don't be ridiculous. You're already inside of me."

With that, she arched into me again, dipping her head and dropping kisses on my neck, little love bites that sent fire spinning in my veins, straight to my already swollen, aching cock. When she shifted her weight slightly, the subtle motion in her channel almost made me come right then.

Dammit all to hell, I couldn't stop this if I tried, and I wasn't just talking about sex. Being inside Shay felt like coming home, and did crazy things to my heart and head. On the heels of a gasping breath, I drove back and sank inside of her, letting myself tumble into the maelstrom of intimacy.

Chapter Twenty-Six

SHAY

With a rough cry, I absorbed the feel of Jackson sinking into me again, his long, thick length filling me completely, the stretch of it intoxicating. I loved the feel of him hard against me, his touch both rough and gentle. My release crashed over me, scattering like sparks, sending me spinning in wave after wave of pleasure, so intense, I could hardly bear it.

He had been relentless, with slow, steady drives into me, ignoring me when I tried to make him go faster. Somehow, he knew that the slow build would make me even crazier and the pleasure even more intense.

I felt the heat of his release filling me as he went taut above me, my name coming in a rough shout. His weight fell against me, and he immediately shifted to the side. It was a small thing, but I loved it. It felt as if he was always making sure he didn't crush me, always thinking about me, whether I needed it or not.

"You're not too heavy," I murmured against his shoulder. He was resting at an angle to my side, still buried inside of me.

His reply was a low chuckle, the warm circle of his palm on my back easing me into sleep within a matter of minutes.

———

The days passed quickly. The lodge stayed busy, with guests coming and going, taking various guided trips daily, and the restaurant was crowded every evening. My weak attempt at lying to myself failed spectacularly. Those nights I tried to convince myself I didn't want to spend with Jackson left me feeling raw, vulnerable, and toeing the edges of uncharted intimacy and hesitant joy. Each night passed—every single one with me falling asleep sated in his arms.

We weren't talking about it, yet we weren't resisting the wild storm of desire that had swept us up. I kept reminding myself every day that I had no expectations.

In all honesty, I didn't. I couldn't imagine a man as good as Jackson truly wanting me. I wasn't going to argue the point, not even with myself, that he wanted me on more than a physical level. There was no doubt about his physical desire for me, not even in my doubt-filled, highly insecure mind.

But, I hadn't forgotten Dani's comments about Jackson and relationships. Nor had I forgotten what a mess I was emotionally. Yet, my heart, my oh-so-tricky heart, was starting to want more. To wish that maybe, just maybe, I could have a shot at something like romance. A shot at having a man like Jackson—or rather, specifically Jackson—who loved me.

That was a very dangerous place to go in my mind. To combat my crazy wishful thinking, during the waking hours, I threw myself into work. There was always more than enough to do. Just the chores alone in dealing with the rescue barn kept me busy for most of the morning and evening. I tried to spend at least a half an hour every day with Mischief working on training, which was mostly fun, but also lots of work.

I was getting quite attached to him and nervous about asking Jackson if he intended to let someone else adopt Mischief, because I had already seen that the rescues who passed through here didn't always stay. Four dogs had been adopted in two weeks, and we had already filled their spaces.

The rescue barn was divided into two sections. One side was essentially a dog kennel, and the other side held the others. Gloria, who Jackson had assured me was a permanent resident, was loose most of the time, although she slept in her own stall. Squeaky could also meander around on her own. The goats wanted to, but they ate everything in their path, so they occasionally shared the pasture with the horses and had their own smaller area to graze.

Jackson was busy too, running from sunup to sundown every day. The only time I saw him, or frankly anyone else, relax was when the staff had dinner together. Even then, that didn't include the staff working in the lodge restaurant. While Dani managed the restaurant staff, she usually found time to take a break for dinner with us.

When I had some free time early one evening, I headed over to help Dani because she told me anytime I needed something to do, to just come find her. She set me to work, helping her prep bread for baking. While we were kneading dough, she glanced over, her gaze speculative. "So, how's it going, being shacked up with Jackson in that cabin?"

My cheeks got hot, and I wished I didn't flush so easily. Glancing up, I lifted a shoulder in a small shrug. "Fine."

Fine didn't quite capture the reality that every night with him was the best sex of my life, but I didn't know how much more I should say.

Dani paused and rested a hand on her hip, cocking her head to the side. "I think something's up. That man can't keep his damn eyes off you."

I took a deep breath and met her gaze, my cheeks getting even hotter. "I'm not sure what to say," I finally said.

"Well, if you're worried about telling me that you two are burning up the sheets, you don't need to worry about that. It's plain as day with the way you look at each other."

By this point, I was concerned my face might actually catch fire. I looked down at the ball of dough under my hands and muttered, "Oh, okay." Gathering my nerve, I looked back to Dani and chewed on my bottom lip. "I don't know what to do. This thing is just happening. I've known Jackson forever, and..." Pausing, I shrugged. "Well, it's not like you don't know I have more than enough baggage. And from what you said"—I lifted my hand, letting it fall to the table—"so does he. This whole thing is crazy. And it's really hard to manage it in the same bed together. There's not even a couch in that cabin."

Dani threw her head back with a laugh. "No, there's not."

I laughed along with her, the heat receding from my face. "Yeah, I think the sensible thing is for us not to be sharing the same bed."

"Why is that sensible?" Dani's question was teasing but earnest.

I shrugged, carefully rolling the dough into a smooth ball and placing it in an oiled bowl before starting on another batch of dough. "Look, even aside from the abuse, my last relationship was a disaster. It's the only serious relationship I've ever had, so I don't exactly have much experience."

Dani stopped rolling the dough she had been working on, setting the rolling pin down and resting her knuckles on the counter. Her gaze met mine across the stainless steel table. "Aside from what you told me, I knew a little about you. We're both from the area, so it wasn't like I had no idea who you were. With Clint Glover's dad being a bigwig in North Carolina politics, the downfall of his son was splashed all over the news. Not that it matters now, but I felt so awful for you. It wasn't just what you went through, but that it was all over the news."

Although I was often hit with random waves of emotion, when it came to Clint, there was a resigned weariness inside. I had cried enough over that man. I carried a sense of shame and worthlessness from ending up in the situation. But it was over, and I was relieved to be out of it.

"Thanks. I know some people still think I lied. I know if there hadn't been a witness in that parking lot that night, Clint probably never would've even been charged for assaulting me."

My mind spun back to the recollection of that woman's comment to Jackson at the vet clinic last week. I still had twinges of discomfort over that, wondering how many people knew I was here and had opinions about me.

Dani's warm gaze held mine. "So that's over. Obviously, you have baggage, but don't we all? I don't see why you should let that stand in the way of maybe this thing with Jackson being something real."

My heart leapt, beating wildly in my chest for a moment, a hopeful bird trying to fly out of its cage. I ignored it. "I don't know. There's all my own stuff, and like you pointed out, Jackson has his. He's distant during the day, and I think he prefers it that way. I can't be falling for some guy where I want more than he does. And I don't really have any clue how to do this. Clint was my only relationship, and I was a virgin until him." Emotion welled up in my throat, and I closed my eyes.

I heard Dani's footsteps rounding the table and then she was beside me, pulling me into a hug. I took a deep breath, letting it out in a muffled sigh against her shoulder.

"I don't usually fall apart like this."

She drew back, squeezing my shoulders, her eyes warm and understanding, with no judgment there. "Of course you don't. But it's okay to fall apart every now and then. Plus, I don't think a few tears counts as actually falling apart."

Stepping away from me, she walked through the back of the kitchen, returning with two wine glasses and a bottle of red wine. The wine was from Lost Deer Winery, a new winery nearby, opened by the family who owned Lost Deer Bar.

Dani and I had determined this new red wine was our current favorite. "It's almost dinner time. We'll finish the bottle," she said with a grin before filling my glass and returning to the opposite side of the table with her own glass.

I had gathered myself together inside and focused on kneading the dough, the rhythmic activity easing the tension tightening inside of me.

Of course, because Dani wasn't one to let a topic drop, she circled back. "So, I suppose my question should've been, what's wrong with being insensible? I'm not asking for details—because I don't actually want to know—but I'm guessing things are good between the sheets with Jackson." My cheeks were red hot in an instant. "Far as I'm concerned, just have a little fun. Good Lord. That man is work, work, work. He's got a heart of gold and he's a good friend, but he almost never takes a break." She paused to take a sip of wine.

"Fun is great and all, but it's kind of complicated. It's not just my baggage, but my brother..."

Dani rolled her eyes, hard. "I know your brother and Jackson are besties and all that, but your brother has no say in your sex life. We are *not* living in the dark ages."

"Oh, I know. But, you know it's a thing. Much as I love Remy, after what happened with Clint, he worries about me. He tries not to make it obvious, but it's totally obvious."

Dani laughed softly, carefully cutting with a cookie cutter into the rolled sheet of dough she'd created. "I'm sure he does. Remy's that kind of guy. I'll leave it at this. Sex aside, I think Jackson likes you. Like, *likes* you."

"Think you could say 'like' one more time?" I teased.

Dani stuck her tongue out at me and took a sip of wine. "You know what I mean."

"You're all about everybody else's love life," I observed, having actually listened to her share her opinions on other's love lives. "What about yours?"

Dani narrowed her eyes, piercing me with a teasing glare. "I don't need a love life. I'm too bossy, and I like to be in control. I guess it's a good thing I know that about myself."

I hadn't missed the few heated moments between her and Wade. It wasn't lost on me there was an electric chemistry between those two. But having had enough of pushing when people weren't ready, I wasn't about to push the issue just now. Despite Dani's declaration that she was bossy and controlling, which I wasn't going to dispute, I sensed an uncertainty and vulnerability for her with Wade. I also sensed there was a story there. Maybe someday I would get it.

Chapter Twenty-Seven

JACKSON

I leaned my back against the door. I had just finished a long day of appointments in the vet clinic. I loved the work, but it meant spinning from one thing to the next for hours. I was out of sorts today too. After those five nights with Shay, five nights of searing intimacy, and, frankly, sex hot enough to burn me to ashes, the guests who had been staying in the farmhouse left. As planned, we returned to the house.

I didn't even want to think about the fact I spent a solid hour contemplating what excuse I could come up with that meant Shay and I needed to remain in that tiny cabin. Everything that wasn't supposed to happen was happening. Shay had sliced through my defenses so easily. She had me off-balance and scrambling for purchase inside.

Just as I had said that very first night, it was crazy for us to act on this desire. And then, when it happened, I tried to talk myself into the reality that it was just chemistry, just attraction. It would burn up and fade. Unfortunately, that wasn't happening. Every taste of Shay only made me want more.

I wanted to be buried inside of her every fucking night of

my life. I wanted to fall asleep with her body warm and soft against mine, and wake up the same way every single day. I wanted sunrises and sunsets, and to never see those flickers of fear that occasionally shadowed her eyes.

I wanted to be her fucking hero, and I was too broken to be that. She didn't know it, but I still had nightmares occasionally. During one of the nights at the cabin with her, I had woken, my heart pounding and my muscles tense. The dreams were strange, and they were rarely clear. They were usually just a jumble of flashes, more comprised of a mix of fear and grief than anything else.

When I startled awake and felt Shay there beside me, she shifted against me with her hand sliding down my side. I had relaxed easily and fallen quickly back to sleep. Although the dreams had lessened in frequency, going from several times a week to just a few times a year, before the other night, there had not been a single night where I actually fell back asleep when I woke from one.

I sure as hell couldn't be her hero, not when I needed her.

"Fuck," I muttered to myself as I pushed away from the door.

I had gotten myself into a hell of a mess. I needed to tell her we had to stop this. But I couldn't bear it. I also needed to talk to Remy. Although I wasn't worried about Remy getting involved with my little sister, seeing as he was in Alaska and nowhere near Ash, I would've wanted him to tell me if our situations were reversed.

Perhaps I was a bit old-fashioned, but it didn't sit right with me to let things play out this far without letting Remy know something.

For all I knew, after everything Shay went through and what Remy knew about me—which was that I had no intention of getting serious with anyone—he'd probably fly home for the sole purpose of kicking my ass. With a mental shake, I stepped to the computer on the counter running along the wall in the small examination room. I clicked into the charts to make sure everything was taken care of for the day, and logged off.

I stepped into the hallway, pausing when I heard Shay's voice filtering down toward me. She was clearly still in her office. She had more than capably taken the reins of all of the administrative tasks. She tidied up my schedule, organized the orders for everything and, according to Dani, was about to take over the scheduling system for the lodge as well.

"On the subject of my love life, I was thinking of entering a convent."

Her tone was teasing, but I knew her well, and I heard the underlying tension and resignation underneath. I was inexplicably furious. Not with Shay, but with her fucking ex, who not only nearly killed her but had taken so much more from her. I wanted to walk in there and show her everything she deserved.

I missed part of her next comment, picking up halfway through. "Hey, I'm just being realistic. My dating prospects are abysmal..."

I forced myself to walk quietly the other way, busying myself by tidying up a few shelves in the storage room. Not for a second did I manage to kid myself that I was doing anything other than waiting for her to get off the phone. I managed to mostly not eavesdrop until I stepped back into the hallway.

"Absolutely. Love you, Remy. I gotta go," I heard her say. There was a pause, and then a goodbye.

I didn't even care to hide the fact I had heard part of her conversation. I strode quickly toward her office, stopping in the doorway. Anger and a depth of emotion only Shay could elicit were tangled together inside as I looked at her.

She spun around in her chair. Her dark blonde hair was up in a messy bun with a pencil stuck through it. Her green eyes were bright, even from across the room. I wanted to kiss her, I wanted to fuck her and make love to her, I wanted to hold her in my arms and tell her she deserved everything.

She looked at me, her gaze slightly puzzled. "Are you okay?" she asked as she stood from her chair and rounded her desk.

"A convent?"

Shay's eyes narrowed, and she twisted her mouth to the side, biting the inside of her cheek as she looked at me. "I was joking," she finally said. "Mind filling me in on why you were listening to my conversation with Remy?"

Stepping into her office and leaning against the wall by the door, I tried to beat back the emotion knotting me up inside. With her gaze on me, I felt the air come alive around us. A riff of sensation chased down my spine.

Only Shay could do this—twist me up inside, make me want things, make me wish I could be the man I wasn't.

"I didn't hear your whole conversation, Shay," I finally managed. "I just heard that last bit when I stepped out of my office."

Her gaze softened, and she nodded slowly, lifting her hands to spin the pencil in her hair. When her bracelet caught on a loose lock, she dropped her hands and sighed. "Dammit." She pulled the pencil out, letting her hair fall loose.

My discipline snapped, and my body reverberated. I half-expected an audible sound from it, the sensation was that intense.

"Are you sure you're okay?" she asked as she tossed the pencil on the desk behind her. Perhaps a few feet separated us. My heart thudded hard inside my chest, and that tangle of emotions held fast. I told her this was crazy, stupid crazy. It still was. Yet, it didn't change how I felt. My emotions didn't seem inclined to listen to reason. I knew precisely why she said the things she said.

I wished I could wipe her ex off the face of the fucking earth. Knowing he was locked up was cold comfort and not enough of a punishment for what he had done to her. Shay deserved so much fucking more, and I wanted to be the man to give it to her.

In a flash, I reached out, catching her hand in mine and reeling her close. She bumped up against me, a surprised little gasp escaping.

"Not really," I murmured, belatedly answering her question. Then, I tangled my hand in her hair and fit my mouth over hers, pulling her flush against me.

I wasn't thinking clearly, at all. Our kiss was rough, hot, and wild. For a moment, she tensed inside my arms before she tumbled into the fire with me. My cock was achingly hard, notched at the apex of her thighs. In a matter of seconds, my hands were roaming her body, one sliding up to cup a breast, another palming her ass as I pulled her tight against my arousal.

We'd been together enough now that I could anticipate her reactions and knew what she liked. She kissed wildly, throwing herself into it. Her tongue was like silk against mine, our kisses sliding into a dark, wet, and deep intensity.

She loved little nips on her neck, so I drew my mouth free, following along her jawline and catching her earlobe in my teeth. I savored her soft cry and the goose bumps under my lips as I made my way down her neck.

I was tugging at her clothes roughly, too tied up inside to slow down, to think maybe I was being too rough with her. Her shirt was thrown on the floor and her jeans kicked off. In a blur, she freed my cock from my jeans, the silky feel of her palm curling around it eliciting a low growl from me.

With her held in my arms, I spun around, striding to the desk and knocking anything in the way to the floor, the loud clatter of it barely puncturing my awareness. All I knew was I needed to be inside of her.

With her warm hands sliding up under my shirt and her bare legs curling around my waist, I fisted my cock in my hand and dragged it through her slick folds. She was already ready, but then, she always was.

I thrust inside of her quickly, burying myself to the hilt. It felt so good, so right. This connection with Shay, as close as I could physically be, caught at the ragged edges inside of me, both tearing and soothing them at once.

The way I felt about her scared the hell out of me. I didn't know what to do about it, all I knew was *this*—her lips touching mine, her tongue slicking against mine, her gasps and cries echoing in my ear when I drew back to fill her again.

There was nothing but the sound of our ragged breathing mingling with the subtle shift of my hips against hers in the room. She took every surge, every breath, every stroke into the core of her.

I was normally a quiet man in passion, but Shay shredded every part of me. I heard myself murmuring dirty pleas, sexy words, rough endearments. All the while, fucking her quick and dirty on the desk.

It was rough, fast, and messy. I felt her tighten, her channel throbbing and milking my cock as my own release threatened to take me under. Reaching between us, I swirled my thumb over her swollen clit, slippery from her juices. Her channel clamped down, and she cried out sharply. I let go, my release crashing over me.

My forehead fell to hers as I tried to catch my breath. I became abruptly aware I had roughly taken her. "I'm sorry. I didn't mean to be so..." I began, my voice ragged.

"It's okay. I wanted it," she murmured in reply, her speech almost slurred with pleasure.

My head fell into the soft curve of her shoulder, and I breathed in the scent of her, trying to gather myself together. Although my need for her was slaked for the moment, I knew it was only temporary.

That's all it ever was with her.

After a few moments, I felt goose bumps rise on her skin

as my hand passed slowly down her back. Although it was a warm spring evening outside, it was air-conditioned in the clinic, and she was bare naked.

I lifted my head slowly, almost afraid to look at her eyes. Her gaze met mine and the intensity contained within eased my heart. At least I wasn't alone in this madness.

At that moment, her stomach growled. Her cheeks flushed pink and her mouth curled into a rueful smile. "I think I'm hungry."

"Ya think?" I teased. I smoothed a hand over her hair. It was a tangled mess now, what with my hand gripping it so roughly. "You gonna grab dinner down at the lodge?"

She was quiet for a beat, just enough for me to be aware that the wheels had started to spin in her mind. Whatever she was thinking, the only thing she said was, "Of course. Dani said she's making pizza for everyone, and I know she makes really good pizza."

My heart pounded hard in my chest. I didn't want to move away, but it wasn't as if I could stand here, buried inside of Shay in her office forever. Although, the idea held its appeal.

"Let's go then," I replied. I drew back slowly and reluctantly. I helped gather her clothes off the floor, buttoned my jeans, and tucked my shirt back into place, as she got dressed quickly.

I even helped tidy up her desk. "Sorry about that," I said, as I gathered up a messy pile of papers on the floor.

She looked over, her eyes snagging mine. Something passed between us and she shrugged. "I guess we were in a hurry."

Just as I stepped out in the hallway, I realized her office door had been open the entire time. It wasn't that I would've expected anyone to stop by here at this time of day, but it shocked me slightly to realize anyone could've walked in on us in the middle of that.

"Jackson," Shay said from behind me. Glancing back, I

saw she had stopped in the doorway, her hand curled over the edge of the frame.

"What?"

"I think at some point we should talk."

My heart started pounding, an unsettled, rapid beat. I knew she was referring to us and this madness we couldn't seem to stop. But I didn't want to talk about it.

"About what?" I deflected.

She looked at me for a long moment, the setting sun through the window casting across her, gilding her in gold. Her shoulders rose and fell as she took a deep breath and let it out with a slow sigh. "Nothing, I guess."

As we walked over to the lodge through the trees, I knew I had fucked up just now. Yet, I couldn't seem to find the words to reach across the subtle distance I felt her put between us.

Chapter Twenty-Eight

SHAY

Days kept passing, and I continued to fail to do what I promised myself I would do. Something had shifted between Jackson and me in the office the other night. At least, something with Jackson.

With me, it was a slow slide to falling in love with a man I didn't think I could have. When he played dumb and said he didn't know what I wanted to talk about, I knew that no matter what I felt from him, he wasn't ready to give it to me. Seeing as I carried enough self-doubt to share freely with the world and never run out, I knew I needed to take care of myself. I needed to put a stop to the intoxicating, crazy hot sex we kept having night after night. I thought I'd be able to put some boundaries in place with us back in the farmhouse and not trapped in a one-room cabin with a single bed. No such luck.

With that in mind, I headed over to the lodge mid-afternoon. There was usually a lull for Dani around then. I hoped to catch her alone and have a private conversation. Just before I reached the back door to the lodge, I encountered

Gloria. The friendly pig wandered over to me, nudging my knee with her nose.

"Hey, sweetie," I said, as I leaned down and rubbed under her chin.

Gloria made her snuffling sound in greeting, and I reached into my pocket to fetch a small treat. I'd learned to keep a variety of treats in my pockets. Squeaky liked dried fruit slices, and Gloria had a preference for the same sweetened grain treats the horses enjoyed.

After Gloria meandered off, satisfied with a little affection and a treat, I found Dani in the kitchen. She was in the midst of inventorying an order. Boxes surrounded her on the floor, circling her feet.

"Need some help?" I asked as I approached.

Dani looked up from the computer tablet in her hands and nodded. "Absolutely. Your timing is perfect. I've checked off everything, so we can just put everything away in storage," she replied, as she tapped a button on the screen and closed the cover, setting the tablet on the table.

We got right to work. I followed her around, putting everything where she told me. Once we were in a rhythm, I just blurted it out. "I need to move into the cabin. Is that okay?"

I actually managed to surprise her. Her wide eyes swung to me, her mouth falling open.

"Um, what?"

"I need to move into the cabin. Is that okay?" I repeated.

Dani set a bag of flour on the shelf and then turned to face me, leaning her hips against the metal shelving and crossing her arms. "Have you asked Jackson about this?"

"Not yet. I figured I'd make sure the cabin was available. I also don't plan to ask him. I'll just tell him."

My heart was pounding hard and fast, drumming to the beat of my anxiety. Everything in me was screaming not to do this. But I was falling in love with Jackson, and he couldn't even talk to me. Before I got in too deep and had my not-so-strong heart banged up any more than it had already been, I needed to take some steps toward self-preservation.

Dani shook her head and sighed. "That bad, huh?"

My throat was tight with emotion and tears were hot in my eyes. I told myself this would be easy. Much easier than anything I'd been through before. So what if I was falling in love? Jackson wasn't going to beat me up and terrify me. I just needed to create enough distance to regroup. If it turned out it was best for me to leave the lodge, I had a few weeks of pay saved up now and could maybe swing a deposit somewhere.

I was torn up inside because I didn't want to leave them in the lurch. No matter what, Jackson and Ash had offered me a haven when I needed it. Jackson was even more important because he was paying me. He'd let me help in the office, so I didn't feel like I was getting paid for next to nothing.

"Have you tried talking to Jackson?" Dani asked, when I didn't reply to her first question.

"I just told you, I'm not asking him. I'll tell him what I plan to do," I stubbornly repeated.

Dani cocked her head to the side. "That's not what I meant, and you know it. I meant, have you talked to him about the two of you?"

My chest was tight, making it hard to take a deep breath. I tried and failed. "Look, I can't do this. I can't fall in love with him. I really need this place. Maybe, if I just get a little space and we stop having sex, I can think a little more clearly. If that doesn't help, well then, I'll figure out somewhere else to be. If there's one thing I learned after the last couple of years of my life, it's that I have to take care of myself. Because no one else is going to do it for me."

She let out a gusty sigh. "Fucking Jackson. He's such an idiot."

I lifted a shoulder in a small shrug. "Maybe not. For what

it's worth, I'm the one who made the first pass. And I promised him I didn't have any expectations. I still don't. But I can't be stupid about it."

Dani wrinkled her nose, something she tended to do when she was annoyed. I might have only known her for a few weeks, but I felt as if I'd known her much longer. The staff here was tight and functioned like a big, messy family. It was impossible not to be drawn in quickly. She was fiercely loyal to her friends, and a mother hen to everyone. She was the kind of friend who was always there when you needed her.

I held her gaze. "Please don't give Jackson grief about this, okay? That won't help anything. He's done more than enough for me. I need to get some space, so we can just be friends like we were before. No matter what, he gave me the one thing I wanted." I hadn't meant to let that last bit slip out, but whatever.

"What's that?" Dani asked, appearing genuinely curious.

"Well"—I paused, feeling my cheeks heat—"before Jackson, Clint was the only guy I ever had sex with. It was never good, so I wanted something other than bad memories."

Dani's face fell. "I know you said you hadn't had a serious relationship before Clint, but I guess I didn't really think about what that meant. Did he...?"

Her words trailed off, but I knew she wanted to ask the hard question. I didn't particularly want to answer, but hiding it didn't really matter. Well, it mattered, but I guess I was tired of hiding just how bad things had gotten. "Yeah. He did. The same night he finally got charged, I ran out of the apartment after he raped me." My words came out level, belying the fear-stained night.

It was strange how, despite the terror of that last night, which came on the heels of years of occasional violence, it wasn't emotional for me anymore. It was a flat, painful place in my heart. It felt as if the emotion had been wrung dry from it. My emotions were much more worked up over Jackson.

Dani was quiet as she looked at me, her skin pale. "It's not like I didn't have some idea of how awful it was, but I am *so* sorry. No one deserves that," she said softly, reaching out and squeezing my hand, her touch warm and reassuring.

"I know. It is what it is. Anyway, back to my question." I couldn't handle talking but so much about it. It was wearying.

I could tell Dani was not pleased with my question about moving to the cabin. Wrinkling her nose again, she said, "There are no plans for the cabin. We usually leave it open in case we hire on extra staff come summer. If you're still here then, we'll figure something out."

"Okay." Disappointment sliced through me. As strong as I was trying to be, part of me had been hoping she would tell me the cabin was booked for guests soon.

"I still think you should try to talk to him first," she muttered as she returned to shelving items.

"I don't think Jackson is ready to talk. And I'm not in a place to try to push for something, and try to make Jackson want something he doesn't really want."

"He wants you!" Dani burst out.

"Oh, I know he wants me *that* way. But I'm pretty confident he doesn't want the rest of it."

I was saved from Dani trying to persuade me further when Evie came barreling in the back door. "You won't believe this!" she said by way of greeting. Striding over to us, she crossed her arms and leaned her head back to glare at the ceiling.

"What the hell did the ceiling do to you?" Dani asked.

Evie brought her gaze to us. "Dawson is pissing me off. He hid all my laundry. Again."

Dawson loved to play practical jokes. Evie was a favorite target because he could wind her up pretty easily. As far as I could tell, she totally had a thing for him and maybe, just maybe, he returned the favor. It was hard to tell with him because he was such a tease. Plus, Evie had a bit of an attitude and knew how to get under his skin.

Dani laughed softly and opened a box of balsamic vinegar, carefully placing the bottles on the shelf.

"Instead of getting pissed off at him, why don't you return the favor?" I asked.

"Or better yet, why don't you two put the rest of us out of our misery and finally have sex?" Dani added.

Evie snorted. "As if. I don't think so. Dawson is totally not my type. Plus, he gets around, and I'm not interested in joining the club."

Dani rolled her eyes. "Sure seems like he's your type when you're staring at him."

Evie quickly turned the tables. "I never said he wasn't hot. Just not my type of hot. While you're busy telling me who I need to get out of my system, why don't you and Wade seriously put the rest of us out of our misery?"

Dani's cheeks flushed slightly, and she rolled her eyes so hard they practically fell out of her head. "As if."

At that moment, the kitchen phone rang, and Dani hurried to get it. By the time she returned, Evie was telling me about her older brother Mack, who was apparently moving back to the area soon.

Evie hung out with us for a bit until we were done putting everything away. Afterwards, I returned to the house. Jackson was in Asheville all afternoon and wouldn't be back until later. I intended to be in the cabin tonight when he got home. I planned to leave him a friendly note and put the ball firmly in his court.

Chapter Twenty-Nine

JACKSON

I rolled my head from side to side, trying to ease the tension bundled in my neck and shoulders. It had been a long afternoon and evening. I'd gone to Asheville to meet with our accountant, which was never my favorite thing to do, and then took care of a long list of odds and ends types of errands.

When I turned into the drive leading to the farmhouse, I saw the lights on in the hallway and the kitchen. My heart started pounding and a little buzz of anticipation spun through me, knowing I was about to see Shay.

When I stepped inside, the house was quiet, so I wondered if she was already upstairs. I fully intended to slip between the sheets with her. My cock stirred at the mere thought of it. Instead, when I glanced in the kitchen, a large piece of paper was sitting on the counter. Before I even got to the counter, my gut was churning and the pounding of my heart had shifted to an erratic beat.

Jackson, I hope your day went well. Your schedule is all set up tomorrow at the clinic. I decided it was best if I moved into the cabin. I promised you I had no expectations. I still don't. But that doesn't mean I'm not falling in love with you. I didn't plan this. I certainly didn't expect it. Things are complicated enough as it is. Since every time I try to talk, you somehow manage to avoid it, I can take a hint.

No expectations and no pressure. But, I'm a bit of a mess all on my own, and I don't want to make things even worse. A little space will probably be good for both of us. I don't have much discipline when it comes to you, so I'm just being honest about it. Above all, you're my friend. I don't want to screw that up.

Offering to let me stay here was a gift you can't even imagine. So I don't want to screw that up too.

You know where to find me if you want to talk. Otherwise, let's fake it until we make it.

Xoxo

Shay

"No," I said to the silent room.

I turned and started to walk down the hallway, with every intention of going to the cabin to find Shay. I went straight there, jogging through the trees. There was no quick way to get there by car, since the cabin was along a trail out behind the main lodge.

Pounding on the door, I called, "Shay, it's Jackson. Let me in."

Silence greeted me.

Reaching for the knob, I twisted it, only to find it locked. She didn't fucking answer.

I didn't get a lick of sleep that night. Dawn rolled around, and I rose. Frustrated, I hoped to run into Shay at the vet clinic or the rescue barn. Instead, I encountered Evie in the rescue barn. If she knew what was up, she didn't let on.

"What the hell are you doing here?" I asked, probably not too nicely.

Evie looked up from where she was filling one of the

dog's food bowls, tossing her braid off her shoulder as she straightened. "Shay texted me and said she had a migraine," she said apologetically.

"Oh. Well, thanks for helping out." I stomped off.

Knowing Shay wasn't working today, I checked on the horses before heading to the lodge for breakfast. Dani had fresh coffee and food ready, and the table had the usual hodgepodge of whoever happened to be up early.

There was no sign of Shay. I got through breakfast with minimal conversation. As soon as I was done, I went to find Shay at the cabin to check on her.

Dani caught up with me just outside the lodge. "Jackson!" she called from behind me.

Turning back, I asked, "What?"

"Well, I know nobody pissed in your cereal because I know what you had for breakfast. What the hell is wrong with you?"

"Shay fucking moved into the cabin," I blurted out, running a hand through my hair in frustration.

Dani rested a hand on her hip. A breeze gusted through the trees, blowing her curls a little wild. "She did. Why does that matter to you?"

My heart was beating hard and fast, a sick, restless beat. My brain felt like it was going to explode. Dani was a good friend—the best kind of friend, really. We'd known each other long enough that she knew when not to push. Right now, I wanted her to do what she did best. She was a problem solver.

I closed my eyes, taking a deep breath in a futile attempt to get this sick feeling to stop churning in my gut and my heart to stop pounding so hard it hurt.

"I just want to talk to her," I finally said, opening my eyes.

"According to Shay, she tried to talk to you. I'm willing to give you the benefit of the doubt that maybe she didn't try that hard," Dani said, rather pointedly.

I breathed in slowly, my frustration about to boil over. "She sure as hell didn't tell me she was planning to pack her shit up and move to the cabin, if that's what you mean by talking to me."

Dani pursed her lips and hummed slightly. "Did she try to talk to you before then?"

After we returned to the house from our heated nights at the cabin, she had told me "*we need to talk*" on three separate occasions. Each time, I remembered the look in her eyes vividly—that vulnerability, front and center, worry flickering in the mossy green depths.

Each time, in all honesty, I'd sidestepped her and blown it off. I hadn't even let the conversation go further than that.

I knew precisely why. The way I felt about Shay scared the hell out of me. She meant too damn much. I couldn't even bear the thought of letting her in further because I knew life and how fucking fickle it was. I couldn't even tolerate the idea of losing her.

When I met Dani's gaze and saw the warm understanding in her eyes, I closed my eyes and shook my head. "I can't do this," I said, spinning away from her and stalking back through the trees, ignoring her when she called my name.

As it was, I was almost late for my first appointment with an adorable long-eared bunny named Fred. Fred's owner was Misty. She was quite beautiful. Once upon a time, not long after I moved back to the farm, she flirted outrageously with me. At the time, I'd sidestepped her fast because she had commitment stamped all over her. She was looking for someone, anyone, to give her a taste of a life outside of this valley. A few years back, her mother was injured in an accident and Misty took care of her.

I managed to skid into the clinic on time. Not much later, I stroked my hand over Fred's soft gray back and glanced across the examination table at Misty. "He's doing just fine." Looking back down at Fred, I cocked my head to the side. "You're the most spoiled rabbit I know. I hope you know that, buddy."

Fred answered with a wiggle of his nose, his whiskers flickering in the air.

Misty smiled over at me. "Thanks, Jackson. How you been?"

Ever since I'd made it clear I wasn't interested, she tempered her flirting, but she was always testing the waters. Looking at her across the table, I tried, I fucking tried, to elicit some sort of interest in her. Not that I intended to do anything about it. I was hoping for even the slightest glimmer to tell me I wasn't doomed for Shay, and Shay alone, forever.

Nothing, not a goddamn thing. In fact, all it did was make my heart squeeze painfully in my chest. Shay had ruined me. I couldn't even imagine being with anyone else after her. Because no one would ever, could ever, measure up. Not even close.

"Doing just fine, you? How's your mama?" I asked.

She shrugged, not even bothering to smile. "Hanging in there."

After Misty left, I had one appointment after another. In between, I found myself checking down the hall to see if Shay showed up. Not so far. I started to wonder if she really did have a migraine. Of course, that got me worried about her.

I was done with my appointments by mid-afternoon and was finishing up when I heard footsteps in the hallway. My heart beat out a hard thump of hope.

Instead of Shay when I looked around the doorway, it was Dawson. I didn't realize I had actually sighed out loud until Dawson stopped in front of me. "Geez, man, that bad to see me?"

I rolled my eyes. "No, just a long day. What brings you over here?"

Dawson leaned a shoulder on the wall, hooking his hand

in a pocket. "Got a call. They need two of us. We're on call, so I figured we'd ride over together. Figured it was just as fast for me to drive here, instead of you driving to pick me up."

"Fuck," I muttered.

"Damn, you're just a ray of fucking sunshine today."

I bit back my next sigh and stepped into the examination room. "Hang on. Let me shut this down, and we'll go."

As I talked, I tapped save on the computer. Shrugging out of the loose scrubs I'd worn over my T-shirt, I tossed it in the laundry bin in the corner and grabbed my bag of gear on the way out.

"What's the call about?" I asked, once we were in the car and on the way.

Dawson, blessedly, offered to drive. Seeing that I was cranky, that was probably for the best. He threw the light on top of the truck and hauled ass. "Climbing accident. Sounds like one of them fell when they were rappelling. The other is stuck on a ledge above."

"Got it. Who's meeting us there?"

"Chief and Lucas. Even though he's not on call, Lucas was at the station dropping off some gear when the call came in, so he volunteered to go with Chief."

"Good. He's solid."

A short drive later, Dawson pulled off into the parking area at the trailhead. This was a popular area for day hikes with a few good rock climbing spots. The area's ease of accessibility meant we were often called here. Inexperienced climbers frequently tried these climbs when they really shouldn't.

Dawson and I threw on our gear and headed up the short hike. When we arrived above the ledge in question, Chief radioed to let us know he and Lucas would be there any minute. The lodge was closer than the station to this area.

"We're not gonna know what we're dealing with until one of us goes down first. I'll start," I offered.

Dawson nodded, quickly pulling out our climbing gear. After we were both in our harnesses, he threaded the line through one of the permanent anchors and glanced to me. "You ready?"

"All set."

I eased over the ledge and started rappelling down slowly, bouncing lightly with my feet on the cliff face as Dawson lowered me down at a slow, steady pace. I didn't climb much for fun anymore, but I loved it. There was something about the focus required that freed my mind. Although my attention was where it needed to be, Shay still lingered in the back of my thoughts. I eased down to the first ledge where I could lean over and look.

From there, I could see one of the two climbers in question. Although it was late afternoon, we had plenty of light left, and I could see the man. "How you doing down there?" I called over.

The man looked up. "I'm okay. I definitely broke my leg," he called up.

I could see climbing rope in a pile beside him. "Where's your climbing partner?"

I couldn't see his expression, but I could hear the worry in his voice. "She slipped and fell below," he replied.

"Hang tight, I'll be down to meet you in a second. We have another team on the way for more help."

I tapped the radio button on my shoulder, calling up to Dawson. "All right. The guy's okay. He thinks he broke his leg. Tell Chief we need another crew. We'll need enough of the team to get him lifted. I don't have much of an update on his partner. When I get down to him, I should be able to see her. If I need to rappel down further, that's what I'll do."

"Got it," Dawson replied. "Giving you more rope now."

Within minutes, I eased onto the ledge beside the man. All I had to do was look at his lower leg to know it was broken. With it being spring, he was wearing fitted climbing shorts. The swelling and odd angle of his tibia were obvious at a glance.

I was relieved that was the situation because it meant we could lift him in a sling and wouldn't need to keep him level on a stretcher. That required a lot more work and more people.

"How's your pain?" I asked.

"Just a dull ache. I'm more worried about Jane," he said when I met his gaze. Based on the look on his face, I knew they weren't just climbing buddies.

"What happened?" I asked.

His voice was thick with emotion when he replied. "I don't fucking know. I don't know what the hell happened. I heard her cry out, and that was the last I heard. I'm scared."

"I'm gonna go take a look, okay?"

"Do you want me to help with the rope?" he asked.

"All set. You're better off to stay put. I could free climb this if I had to. I'm on a long damn rope, so my guy up above can still manage it."

After threading the line through the anchor on this ledge, I continued my descent. This next drop wasn't too far. Easing over the ledge, I looked down to see the woman in a crumpled ball on the ground below. It was no more than thirty feet down. I hoped like hell she was alive.

Once again, Shay strolled into my thoughts. Now was *not* the time to have a deep conversation about love with the man sitting up above me, but based on the look in his eyes, I surmised he loved Jane.

Right about now, I didn't give a damn what I was afraid of. I was most afraid of not having a chance to make sure Shay knew exactly how I felt.

Chapter Thirty

JACKSON

I forced my thoughts off of Shay and kept my attention on my slow descent to the ground below. I landed lightly on firm ground and immediately leaned over to check the woman's pulse. It was shallow, but steady. I breathed a sigh of relief and called up, "She's okay."

"Oh, thank God," the guy above called back. "Jane!"

Of course, she couldn't reply. My heart clenched. I replied, "She has a pulse, but she's not conscious."

I took a few moments to check her carefully. Aside from the lump on the back of her head, she seemed okay. In another moment, I heard more voices above me. Relieved, I radioed up. Dawson's voice came through. "Chief sent me down with Lucas. We're going to get this guy in a sling and then I'll meet you down there. What are we looking at?"

"Aside from a knot on the back of her head, I can't see any other injuries. Looks like her harness came loose."

This wasn't too long of a fall, although if she had fallen the wrong way, we could've been dealing with a much more difficult situation.

"Got it. I'll be down in a few."

Now, I just needed to wait. I settled down on the ground beside Jane. I hoped like hell she was just knocked out from hitting her head. After a few moments, she murmured something.

Her eyes blinked open, and I breathed a silent sigh of relief.

"Matt?" she asked, her tone confused.

"I'm not Matt, but he's okay. I'm Jackson. How are you feeling?"

She started to sit up quickly. "Take it easy," I said.

"What happened?" she asked, swinging her gaze to me.

"Looks like your harness clip broke, and you fell. You didn't fall far. Before you move too much, let me do a few quick checks. Tell me how many fingers I'm holding up."

She sighed, but answered obediently. "Three." I held up two more. "Five." I held up a single one. "One."

"Tell me what day of the week it is."

"Friday."

"Where are you?"

"In the Blue Ridge Mountains."

"Any dizziness?" I asked, as she attempted to sit up again.

"A little bit, and I feel a little sick," she said, wrapping an arm over her belly. "Are you sure Matt's okay?"

"He broke his leg, but otherwise, he's fine."

I tapped my radio. "Hey guys, status?"

"Just about to lift him up in the sling," Lucas replied.

"Got a minute to let him hear his girl's voice?"

"Oh yeah," Lucas said.

He must've leaned over for the radio to be near Matt's mouth because Matt's voice came through clear as a bell. "You okay, Jane?" he asked.

"I'm fine, just a little dizzy." A tear rolled down her cheek. "How's your leg?"

"Broken," he said with a laugh. "I'm just glad you're okay. I love you."

"You two are going to see each other soon as we get you

both up there. We've already got an ambulance waiting." Lucas's voice came through the speaker. "Let our guys do the work. Dawson'll be down in a few," Lucas added.

Jane promptly burst into tears.

"Ah, everybody's okay," I said, rubbing my hand on her back. "Matt's a little banged up, and it sounds like you gave your head a good knock. But you're both going to be fine."

Now that the urgency was past, all I could think was I needed to get the hell back home and talk to Shay.

In short order, we had them loaded into the ambulance and headed to the hospital. The EMT crew took over from there. Once we were in the truck, I glanced to Dawson. "I got a call to make. You mind?"

"Who?" Dawson countered because he was nosy as hell.

"Shay's brother, and my best friend."

"Sure thing," Dawson replied with a grin.

"Only because this can't wait," I muttered.

Fishing my phone out of my bag on the floor, I pulled up Remy's number and tapped the call button.

He answered right away. "Hey, Jackson, what's up?"

"Well, I was calling to talk to you about Shay."

I figured there was absolutely no point in dancing around this and dove right in.

"Is she okay?" he asked quickly, the concern more than evident in his voice.

"Oh, she's fine, man. I'm just calling to let you know I'm in love with her."

There was a moment of electric silence and then Remy's voice came through the line, his words edged with tension. "What?"

"I'm in love with Shay."

Dawson happened to be coming to a stop at an intersection right then, and cast a wide-eyed glanced in my direction.

"When the hell did this happen?" Remy asked, his tone low.

I knew him well enough to know he was pissed. Perhaps not for me falling in love with his sister, but for reaching this point without him knowing a damn thing about it.

"Since, just since... Hell, I don't know, but now for sure. Look, I'm calling you because I... Well, hell. I didn't plan on this. At all. But I didn't want you to think it was anything other than that. I would never hurt her. You have to know that."

"For fuck's sake, Jackson. You know what she's been through. How do I know you would never hurt her? Let's face it, you've made it clear since you got back that you never had any intention of getting serious. With anyone."

"Remy, I know. With Shay, it's different. Obviously, I know what she's been through. I can't change how I feel."

My throat was tight with emotion and my heart was pounding hard, crashing against my ribs. Somehow, saying it all aloud drove home the point of how real it was.

Remy was quiet long enough that I prompted, "Are you still there?"

"Yeah. Still here. I'm gonna call Shay. You might be my best friend, but you better fucking know that if you hurt a single hair on her head, I'll beat the fucking shit out of you."

"Remy, I get it. You know I would never, *ever* lay a hand on her, right?"

Anger lashed inside. I didn't think that was what he meant, but I needed to make it abundantly clear that would never happen.

"Hell yes, I know that. That's not the kind of hurt I'm talking about."

Leaning my head back against the seat, I let out a breath I hadn't even known I'd been holding. "Okay, man. Just making sure. You know if you call her and tell her I just called you, she's gonna be pissed as hell. I didn't exactly talk to her about this before I called."

"That I do. And I don't give a shit. You can deal with it. If you love her, it won't matter."

At that, he clicked off the line. I slipped the phone into my pocket, shifting in my seat.

"Sounds like that went *real* well," Dawson offered, his tone dry.

Rolling my head to the side, I cast a mild glare him. "Don't give me shit, man."

For a moment, he looked as if he wanted to tease, but his gaze sobered. "It's been obvious to the rest of us she means a lot to you. For what it's worth, I think it's a good thing. Shay's been to hell and back. She deserves a good man," he said, his tone somber.

My mouth dropped open. Dawson, the perpetual tease and flirt, was dead serious. "Uh, wow, that's not what I expected from you."

Dawson lifted his shoulder in an easy shrug as he turned onto the road leading to the farm. "I might tease, but I'm a romantic at heart, man."

I chuckled. I should've expected he would rebound quickly. Much as he liked to play the joker, Dawson was a good guy. I knew the crew here had gotten protective once they got to know Shay. I was grateful for that.

I didn't quite know how to consider his comment that she needed a good man like me. I might be coming to terms with the depth of my feelings and what she meant to me, but I knew it would be a challenge to be the kind of man she deserved.

The rest of the drive was quiet. Although clouds had been threatening for most of the day, it wasn't until the sun began to set that they crowded the sky and it started to rain abruptly, the sound drumming against the windshield and amping up my impatience to get to Shay. My phone vibrated in my pocket after a few minutes. Slipping it out, I saw Shay's number on the screen. Seeing as Remy had flat-out told me he was calling her, I figured that's why she was calling me. I didn't know what to expect, but I wasn't going to be a chicken shit and avoid her call.

Sliding my finger across the screen, I answered, "Hey, Shay."

"How dare you call Remy?!"

"I had to call him, Shay."

"Maybe you could've talked to *me* first about how you feel," she said, her voice ragged. I could hear the tears threatening and wished like hell I was there.

"Shay, let me..." My words went nowhere when the phone went dead in my ear.

I hit redial immediately, only to get her voicemail. She had promptly turned her phone off.

"Trouble in paradise?" Dawson asked, his tone sly.

"Dude, not now. Hit the gas and get me back to the farm so I can find Shay."

Chapter Thirty-One

SHAY

I paced in a small half-circle around the bed in the tiny cabin. I could *not* believe Jackson had called Remy. I was so rattled by Remy's call, my heart was jumping all over the place inside, restlessness and anxiety keeping my feet pacing. For starters, Jackson had no business telling Remy about us. And then he told Remy he was in love with me. So Remy said.

What the fuck? He can't tell me how he feels, but apparently Jackson has no trouble telling my big brother all about his feelings.

Too restless to remain trapped in the small cabin, I looked out the windows. Rain had begun to fall, the sky a dark slate with evening well on its way. I didn't care. I needed to do something. I had already fed all the animals, but I could always check on them. Hurrying out of the cabin, I walked swiftly through the trees, welcoming the cool rain striking against my cheeks. I avoided the path that led to the lodge and hoped no one happened to notice me. Now was about time for dinner and I was in no mood to be social.

Part of me was overjoyed, to the point of giddy tears. Yet

another part of me was completely thrown by Jackson's call to Remy. It chafed to have men make decisions about me. I didn't know what was said during that phone call. All I knew was Remy told me Jackson was in love with me, and Remy wanted to make sure I was okay.

Then, he got all high-handed and went off on some over-protective older brother lecture about making sure to let him know if Jackson hurt me. When I pointed out that Jackson was his best friend and wouldn't ever lay a hand on me, Remy bluntly stated that's not what he meant and assured me he wouldn't stand in the way, as long as Jackson didn't hurt me. As if he had some say in my love life.

I hung up on him.

Passing through the horse barn, intending to stop and say hi to Mischief, I was a little let down to see he was out in the far corner of the pasture. He hated to be cooped up, and I loved that Jackson didn't even try to contain him. His stall was always left open, even when the other horses were up for the night. "Spoiled horse," I murmured to myself.

I cut across the pasture to the far side where the rescue barn was. When I stepped inside, I glanced over at the dogs who respectively lifted their noses to investigate. They were down for the evening in their spacious kennels.

I paused beside one of my current favorites. I loved them all, but I was a softie, and we'd just taken in a rescue over the weekend who was so thin it hurt to look at her. She was nothing more than a skeleton with fur. She was a sweet English setter, abandoned by her owner for reportedly being gun-shy.

Opening her kennel, I paused to stroke her head. She leaned into me, soft and sweet. "Hey, Pepper," I murmured, as she let out a deep sigh. Simply touching her eased the anxious restlessness coursing through me.

After Pepper turned to curl up in her bed again, Gloria meandered over. She was no fan of the rain, so I guessed she'd stayed put since her evening meal. She snuffled, and I gave her a treat before handing out treats to everyone.

I didn't know why I was so out of whack. I should've been happy. I felt strangely bereft and overjoyed at once. It was almost as if I couldn't quite believe Jackson loved me. Considering I was on the verge of trying to look for another living situation, I should've been beside myself.

But it didn't feel quite real. I had thoroughly absorbed the belief that love wasn't something that would come along for me. I truly believed it was enough to be safe, and that expecting anything more from the universe was folly.

I brushed my damp hair out of my eyes and leaned against the wall after Gloria wandered into her stall. It was quiet in the barn, with nothing but the soft sounds of the various animals settling down for the night. I took a deep breath and let it out, just as the door at the back of the barn opened.

Rolling my head to the side along the wall, I saw Jackson entering. He walked with his usual easy confidence, although tension emanated from every step. He hadn't seen me yet. He glanced around, his gaze swinging wildly before it landed on me.

My heart contracted painfully, pounding so hard it felt as if it might fly out of my body.

"Oh, thank fucking God, Shay. I've been looking all over, and you're not answering your phone."

I swallowed through the emotion thick in my throat and managed a shallow breath. Jackson stopped in front of me, his eyes coasting over my face. "You're soaked," he said, his tone gentling. "And you're shivering."

He stepped close, pulling me into the shelter of his arms.

My body was shaking, the tension discharging in rough tremors. "I guess I forgot my phone in the cabin," I mumbled into his chest.

He held me flush against him, one strong arm wrapped around my waist with his hand cupping my bottom and the other around my shoulders. His head bowed beside mine as he breathed me in.

"No wonder I couldn't get a hold of you," he murmured into my hair.

I hadn't realized how chilled I was from the rain until his heat began to seep into me. He smelled good—warm, woodsy, and crisp with a hint of rain.

His hand swept in steady passes up and down my back. "I shouldn't have called Remy until I talked to you. I'm sorry for that," he said, his voice rough.

My heart stuttered and set to pounding hard against my ribcage again. I lifted my head, leaning back slightly to look into his eyes. "It's okay. Remy can be kind of bossy. And I kind of like to feel like I'm in control, at least when it comes to matters that involve me," I said, slightly surprised my words came out.

I didn't realize I was crying until Jackson's eyes narrowed and his brow furrowed. He loosened his hold on me and lifted a hand, swiping the tear away with his thumb.

"I screwed up bad enough to make you cry, huh?"

I shook my head. I didn't know exactly why I was crying. I was mostly overcome with emotion. A giddy sense of joy buzzed through me, mingling with awe at how much it meant to actually fall in love with someone.

"No, it's not that. I'm just..." I couldn't seem to find the words, and another tear rolled down my cheek. Because he was Jackson, and he seemed to understand me in ways no one else could, he didn't insist I try to talk it out. I leaned my head into his chest and tried to collect myself. After a few more deep breaths of his scent, I managed to pull myself together.

Leaning back again, I caught his eyes, this time the sense of joy overriding the rest of my feelings. "So, you called Remy."

His mouth hitched at the corner, a gleam entering his gaze. "That I did. I called him to tell him I'm in love with you. I was ready to deal with him telling me he was going to come out here and kick my ass, but he hung up on me first," he explained with a low chuckle.

"Remy called me."

"You mentioned that. What did he say?" Jackson asked softly. I stared into his eyes, that rich blue gaze ebullient, and my heart so full I could hardly bear it.

"He said he wouldn't stand in the way. I'm not sure if he's planning to come kick your ass though because I hung up on him."

Jackson's grin stretched to the other corner of his mouth. "I'll deal with it if he does."

We stood there for several long moments. Even though my pulse was running wild, a sense of comfort and ease stole through me. I never imagined I would feel this safe with someone. All of my feelings spun into the most intense desire I could imagine with a depth of intimacy running through it like a vein of gold.

When I leaned back again, I saw the question in his eyes. "I moved into the cabin because I knew I was in love with you. I didn't want to make things more complicated than they already were. And I promised you I had no expectations, so..." I got nervous suddenly and bit my lip, worrying it with my teeth.

Jackson threw his head back with a laugh. "Darlin', it's been complicated since the day you walked back into my life. I don't give a damn. I guess it's a good thing I've got my own shit, so I don't worry too much about complications."

We didn't speak of it much, if hardly at all, but I knew Jackson had his own scars to bear. I lifted a hand, tracing my fingers along his jawline and circling his lips.

In a hot second, his lips were on mine. I forgot everything but the feel of his warm mouth working mine, his kiss sweet and hungry, and the feel of his hard body holding me close, sheltering me from the world.

A funny squeak punctured the haze of passion filling my

mind. This time, I knew the sound. Jackson's lips started to blaze a trail down my neck, and I murmured, "We have company."

He lifted his head, arching a brow in question. "We've got more than company. We've got a whole freaking audience here."

I giggled and watched as he drew away slowly, catching my hand in his. He paused to lean over, pulling a treat out of his pocket for Squeaky. It didn't take much to please Squeaky, and she happily chomped on the piece of dried apple he handed her.

In the cool spring rain, we walked back to the farmhouse, and the night was mine and Jackson's alone. He made me crazy, but then, that seemed to be the case whenever we were anywhere near each other.

His hands mapped my body, his lips finding every forgotten corner. When he sheathed himself inside of me in a slow, delicious slide, my release wasn't far away. Pleasure spun through me in hot sparks as he sought his own release.

I woke during the night with him spooned behind me, holding me close. For a flash, I was anxious, fretting over how to relax and fall back to sleep. His hand slid down my side, over the curve of my hip in a soothing stroke, and I realized we had a lifetime to make new memories.

EPILOGUE

Shay

A year or so later

Jackson and I had married in the small outdoor chapel his mother had built years back on the farm. We married the following spring, a full year after I had arrived.

This afternoon, I was returning from an appointment with my doctor. I hadn't told Jackson about it and was now wishing I had. I didn't like to keep any secrets, even small ones that were for a surprise.

Perhaps because both of us had been through some difficult times, the idea of having children had once seemed like an impossible dream. I had carried the knowledge, because of what happened with Clint and injuries I had sustained, that there was a slim possibility I might not be able to conceive.

I found out this afternoon that, while I did have scarring, I should be able to get pregnant. I was anxious to tell Jackson.

Jackson was upstairs in the vet clinic, finishing up his day of appointments. As I walked down the hallway, I heard yet another pet owner flirting with him. This was a common occurrence. I had discovered I was not the jealous type, if only because it bemused me to watch him fend off attention. My lack of jealousy was likely assisted by the fact Jackson couldn't keep his hands off me.

I stepped into my office, wanting to wait for a private moment to greet him. In the past year, I'd settled into my role here. Ash had come and gone a few times, and given her blessing to my relationship with Jackson, as had Remy. He had given me away at our wedding a few months prior.

Meanwhile, I had fully assumed responsibility of all administrative duties for the vet clinic, the rescue program, and the lodge. Everyone was frankly quite relieved, but most especially, Jackson. He hadn't been lying when he said he hated the business side of the work.

I heard him say goodbye and listened as his footsteps came down the hallway. Turning to face the doorway, I found his lazy grin waiting for me. He leaned a shoulder against the door and eyed me. His shaggy brown hair looked as if he'd run a hand through it a few too many times today. It was no wonder women were always flirting with him. The navy T-shirt he wore today brought out the blue of his eyes and didn't do a damn thing to mask his muscled chest and shoulders.

My belly spun in a flip and my pulse skittered wildly. I kept thinking my body's response to him would slow down, but that didn't seem to be the case. If anything, the more time we spent together only deepened our intimacy and desire.

"Hey, darlin'," he said as he stepped through the door, approaching me where I stood by the desk. "How was your day?"

"Good," I murmured softly, a little gasp slipping out when he crowded against me and lifted my hips onto the desk behind me.

Standing between my knees, he shifted me closer, dipping his head to dust kisses along the side of my neck. I'd discovered over the course of the year that Jackson was quite affectionate. In fact, he took every chance he got to manhandle me. I found I didn't mind, not in the slightest. His strength was easy and gentle, always.

"I had an appointment today."

"Oh?"

"It was my annual checkup. Since we've been talking a little bit about kids, I asked my doctor to check and make sure everything was okay." My heart was beating wildly as I got the words out. This made it all feel so real, so concrete. So possible.

Jackson's gaze sobered quickly. "You didn't mention you were even worried," he murmured as he brushed a loose lock of hair away from my forehead, tucking it behind my ear. A little shiver chased across my skin in the wake of his touch.

I was suddenly a little anxious and curled my fingers around the edge of his sleeve, tracing over the curve of his biceps with my thumb. "I didn't know. I was worried a little after everything that happened," I finally said.

Jackson remained the only person who knew the details of everything that happened with Clint, aside from my therapist. She had reminded me that I owed no one my story, that it was in my control to talk about it. He was quiet long enough that I started to worry.

But when I looked up to meet his gaze, I saw nothing but understanding and love shining back. Although his own scars were so different from mine, he understood on a deep level what it meant for me to have gone through what I did and how important it was to handle it on my terms.

"Okay then. All systems go?"

The building tension eased instantly, unspooling rapidly inside. I smiled and lifted a finger to trace along the stubble of his jaw. "Absolutely."

"Oh good. So, when do we get started?"

I grinned, teasing my fingers into his hair along the nape of his neck as I drew him close. "Now."

When his lips met mine, the sensation was electric, sending a hot jolt through my system. *This* man. Only his kisses were enough to singe me on contact.

———

JACKSON

Another six months later

Shay stood before me, her hair falling around her shoulders in a tousle. It was still long enough to reach her waist, although the only chances I got to see it down were times like now, when it fell loose from her usual ponytail, or when I got her naked.

She was a rather practical woman. At the moment, she was laughing as Mischief flicked his tail and trotted off into the pasture.

I opened the gate and stepped into the small paddock from the side. "How'd it go?" I asked as I approached her.

She glanced at me, still smiling. "Let's just say you chose his name well."

I laughed as I caught her hand in mine and reeled her to me. When she came against me, I felt the soft curve of her belly. My mind spun back to a year and a half ago, when she came strolling back into my life.

Only six months ago, we decided to try to start a family. If you had asked me before—even when I was deep into falling in love with Shay—if I thought I wanted to start a family, I would've told you that was crazy. That was when I thought I understood loss. I believed it made life easier if you didn't set yourself up for more pain and grief by letting anyone matter too much.

But then Shay came along, and reminded me—or rather, taught me—how wrong that lesson was. I would feel as if I lost half of myself if I lost Shay, but what we had made everything that much more precious. The sun shone a little brighter in every moment because of her. It wasn't worth it to live half a life.

Although I would never let go of the lingering fury with her ex, she was at peace, and that was all that really mattered. And now, startling us both, she had just passed her first trimester. We had an appointment in a month to find out if it was a boy or a girl. I was worried I'd scar my tongue over the next six months from biting it to keep from telling her to be careful all the time.

This part of loving her nearly killed me. I knew how much it mattered to her to feel in control, so I held my worries close to my chest. For her, I would do anything.

She leaned up, still laughing, and catching my lips in a kiss. In a hot second, I forgot where we were. I threaded my hand in her hair and fit my mouth over hers for one of those hot, hungry kisses that I could *never* get enough of.

When I drew away, she was smiling against my lips. "What?" I asked.

"I think I'll stop riding for now. Even *though*, my doctor says I don't have to. I know it worries you, and Mischief can get a little wild."

My heart was thudding, hard and fast in my chest, the way it did whenever anything reminded me just how much she meant to me.

"Really?" I murmured against her lips, my forehead resting against hers.

"Uh-huh. It's not worth the worry. I might go for a ride on old Cinnamon, but all he does is amble. It's almost too much to ask him to trot. There's plenty to do with Mischief for training without being on his back."

"I won't pretend I'm not relieved," I finally said, sliding my hand over the subtle curve of her belly. To me, it had been obvious she was pregnant since the day the test was positive, but Shay insisted it wasn't that obvious. We finally planned to share the news with everyone else tonight.

Leaning back, she smiled. "Of course you're relieved."

I considered myself an easygoing man. For the most part, I was. Yet, I had discovered that when it came to Shay, she alone had a unique ability to send my heart to a wild, rushing beat, with worry spinning through me.

"Hey," she said, her smile fading slowly. "What's that look for?"

"It's just, you mean so damn much. I can hold it together, right?"

This time, her smile was soft, her green gaze holding mine and reminding me that while I wanted to shelter her, in so many ways, she was everything to me.

"Of course." Her fingertip traced my mouth, then she was tugging me down to her again. "I think we should go to the tack room."

I laughed, lifting her against me as her legs curled around my hips. It was rather convenient that the lodge guests didn't come over to this part of the farm often. Otherwise, we might have to curtail our rather frequent public displays of affection and tendency to run off and get naked wherever we felt like it.

With my girl held tight against me, I dipped my head, nipping softly at the salty skin on her neck. "Love you."

"Love you more," she teased.

Hours later, when we were in bed, the cool autumn air filtering through the windows, Shay's skin was damp against mine. I lay awake, debating whether I needed to schedule an appointment with her doctor and make sure I clarified the limits of sexual activity for a pregnant woman.

Shay had instigated this tonight. After our interlude in the barn. I couldn't say no to her. *Ever*.

———

Thank you for reading This Crazy Love - I hope you loved Jackson & Shay's story!

Up next in the Swoon Series is Wait For Me - Lucas & Valentina's story. It all starts with a package that ends up in the wrong hands. Lucas is a single father who takes tall, dark & brooding to new levels.

Valentina has a problem she'd like to solve. Namely, ditch her virginity. Simple enough, right?

Lucas & Valentina's unlikely romance is hot, hot, hot & oh-so-swoony. Don't miss their story!

Keep reading for a sneak peek!

Be sure to sign up for my newsletter for the latest news, teasers & more! Click here to sign up: http://jhcroixauthor.com/subscribe/

Rounding the corner in the hallway, I ran smack into a wall. A wall that turned out to be a person. With two boxes cradled in my arms and a pile of mail on top of that, everything tumbled to the floor. Flustered, I looked straight up into the dark green gaze of Lucas Cole. If he even noticed I'd just dumped mail all over the floor, he didn't show it.

But that was nothing unusual. Neither was the fact my pulse lunged and my body got hot all over. Lucas had that effect on me, and probably most women. He took that whole tall, dark, and broody thing to heart.

"I'm sorry!" I blurted out. "Let me just get all this ..."

My words trailed off because the bad luck of literally running into him only amped up my flustered state and left me breathless. I leaned over to scoop up the mail and bumped my head into his forearm. Dear God. Since when were forearms that hard?

"No worries," Lucas replied as he handed me the mail he had already gathered.

My fingers brushed his as I took it, causing a zing of electricity to race up my arm. Before I could formulate a response, he leaned over and picked up the two small packages. As he handed them over, my brain fired off a thought.

"Oh, one of these is yours," I said, my words coming out rushed.

Juggling the mail and the boxes, I gave him one box. Lucas took it, hooking it in the bend of his elbow. "Thanks. See you around."

With a brief nod, he continued down the hallway. I remained frozen, waiting until I heard his footsteps recede. At the sound of the door closing behind him, I sagged against the wall. Of all the people to run into, it had to be Lucas.

Lucas worked at Stolen Hearts Lodge like me. He was also the sexiest man I'd ever laid eyes on. I could hardly be near him without my body going haywire, as evidenced by this brief encounter. I knew without a doubt that Lucas was *waaaaay* out of my league.

After several deep breaths, I carried on, dropping off the mail in the office and heading to my cabin.

Climbing the steps, I turned to look behind me. The setting sun cast the mountains in shadow. I didn't linger long, not with the small box in my hands. I'd gotten so frazzled seeing Lucas that I forgot about my own mail until I was almost here.

I let myself into my small cabin. This was the first place I'd lived away from my family, so it was ridiculously awesome for me. With only one bedroom, one bathroom, and a pretty view of the Blue Ridge Mountains, it was tiny, but I loved it. Like *loved* it, loved it.

I set the small square box on my dresser. As I held the thin blade of my pocketknife over it, my eyes landed on the label. My heartbeat lunged, and my belly spun in a nervous flip. I was expecting a package, but this was *not* it. For those of us who worked at Stolen Hearts Lodge, all mail came addressed to the lodge, so it was important to pay attention to the return address. Much too late, I noticed this box had the name of a construction supply company on the return address label.

There was only one other person who had received a package in the mail today. Lucas. I'd handed him the wrong one.

"Oh, shit!"

I clapped my hand over my mouth. I didn't know if I'd ever get over that habit. Despite my parents' best efforts, my mouth had a mind of its own. The issue of having the wrong box was worthy of more than one *oh shit*, though.

"Fuck, fuck, fuck."

If only I could apply that word to something beyond a curse. My complete *lack of* in that area was part of my problem right now. I just gave Lucas Cole a box with …

There was a sharp knock on my door. Startled, I dropped the pocketknife, jumping at the sound of it clattering to the floor. As I leaned over to pick it up, my elbow collided with the corner of the Bible my mother had mailed to me the other day. Like I needed a Bible. The plump book thudded to the floor just as another knock sounded.

My heart was pounding wildly, and I was already about to melt from embarrassment even though I didn't know who was at the door. Not for sure. Ignoring the small mess I'd made on the floor, I squared my shoulders and turned and strode to the door, curling my hand around the knob.

No need to freak out. It's probably not him. On the heels of a deep breath, I opened it and found myself staring into Lucas's green gaze for the second time in an hour.

Shit, fuck, hell, damn.

That was technically only three swear words, and all of them stayed in my brain. You know, like a silent vowel except the entire word was silent. Hell was a place, so it didn't count as a swear. Or so I'd convinced myself at some point during my childhood.

Lucas stood there with an opened box in his hands.

Oh. My. God.

He'd opened the box.

I had the worst luck. Or maybe it was the most embarrassing luck. Was it too much to ask that I have a little dignity around the one man who tended to leave me feeling all swoony and ridiculous?

My eyes, because they were naughty and ignored my mind, meandered over Lucas, taking in his bold features—a strong nose, angled cheekbones, a square jaw with a dark trimmed beard, and sensual lips. Okay, his face was too much. Throw in his to-die-for body—all rangy muscle—and well, I thought God had been a bit too generous in the looks department with Lucas. Just sayin'.

Lucas stared at me quietly, his gaze scanning my face. My cheeks heated the moment I saw his lips quirk with a hint of a smile.

"I think this belongs to you," he said, his voice like sweet sorghum, sliding over me with its slow drawl.

My face was on fire. Hell, it wasn't just my face. *I* was on fire.

"Um, are you sure?" I hedged.

"The address was for the lodge, but it has your name on the receipt in the box," he replied smoothly, losing the battle against his smile.

Not fair! The first time I got to see Lucas smile and it was all because I was an idiot.

"Oh," I replied brilliantly.

He held the box forward, and my eyes—still disobeying me—dropped to look in the box at the hot pink vibrator. It wasn't even hidden. Encased in clear hard plastic, I wouldn't have been surprised if it jumped out of the box and said hello to me, so bold was its presence.

I swallowed and looked back up at Lucas. I couldn't think, much less speak. I now understood how clichés came to be. I was quite certain I might *actually* die of embarrassment. I was hot all over, my pulse had taken off like a rocket

—not joking, it could've propelled me into space—and I felt lightheaded.

Lucas's voice came to me from a distance. "Valentina? Are you okay?"

Nope. Definitely not okay. Everything blurred, and my legs felt wobbly. Then, I fell over.

I seriously fainted in front of Lucas hot-as-sin Cole while he held a box with the vibrator I ordered in his hands.

LUCAS

Valentina Smith stared at me, her blue eyes wide, and her cheeks nearly as pink as the vibrator in the box. I was doing my damnedest to keep my response to her in check, but you have *no* idea how hard that was. Well, some things *were* most definitely hard. Valentina should've come with a warning sign.

She had curly red hair that practically begged for a man to tangle his hands in it, round blue eyes, and cheeks with freckles dusted over them like gold glitter. She was on the short side and had nothing but curves. She was sex and sin with this hint of innocence to her that made me fucking crazy.

To deal with my out-of-control response to her, I generally ignored her. However, when I tore open this little box and discovered what was inside, holy fucking hell, I had no choice but to come return the package to her. Any other alternative involved someone else, and I could only imagine the less people involved, the better.

It was as if I could hear the beat of time ticking as we faced each other. I gathered she was a bit embarrassed about the situation. Hence, my reason for delivering this personally. Or so I told myself.

My eyes dropped down to the box, and I bit back a chuckle. When I opened the box and saw that vibrator staring back at me, my mouth fell open. I'd been expecting a box with new work gloves. Far more boring than this. I didn't doubt any woman would find satisfaction from this thing. It appeared to have quite a few bells and whistles.

When I looked back at Valentina, her eyes were hazy. I could see the wild flutter of her pulse in her neck and realized she might be about to faint.

"Valentina? Are you okay?"

As I reached over to steady her, she wobbled slightly before collapsing. Fortunately, I caught her by the arm, letting the box fall to the floor as I wrapped my arm around her waist. She was completely out.

I lifted her limp body into my arms and carried her over to the bed, the only obvious option at the moment. There wasn't even a couch in here. It was either the bed or the floor.

Although alarm bells were blaring in my mind—because me, Valentina, and a bed weren't a great plan—I eased her down gently. I quickly checked her pulse to find it was shallow but steady.

I adjusted the pillows under her head and rested my hips on the edge of the bed. Part of me wanted to simply leave at this point. Not because I wanted to leave Valentina after she fainted, but rather, to escape this crazy sense of protectiveness she elicited from me.

With that tangling up in my body's always instantaneous response to her, I needed to be careful. Very careful.

I lifted a hand and brushed a few of her wild red curls away from her forehead, resting the back of my hand against it briefly. Her skin was cool and clammy under the flushed surface.

As a first responder, my instincts to check on things like that were automatic. Her breaths came in shallow pants, and after a few moments, her eyes opened slowly.

"Well, there you are," I commented, unable to keep from smiling.

Whether it was in relief or this strange sense of joy I

experienced being near her, I didn't know. That odd feeling of joy didn't make a lick of sense. Not right now. She had just fainted, for God's sake. I knew she was fine, but still. Her eyes focused on me, slightly confused.

"What happened?"

"You fainted."

She rose on her elbows, her skin turning pink again. "I fainted?"

"Most definitely."

"Did I fall?" she asked as she pushed herself back up on the pillows, looking around.

My eyes lingered on the smatter of haphazard freckles on her cheeks and dropped to the tempting dimple in the center of her plump bottom lip. As she sat up, her T-shirt stretched tight across her generous breasts. I couldn't help but notice the press of her nipples through her bra and the thin cotton shirt.

Dude. What the hell are you doing? She just fainted in front of you, and you're staring at her breasts.

I can't help it. They're near perfect.

That was how bad I had it. My internal debate had a point. I didn't like to think about it, but I had wondered more than once just how her curves felt.

"Lucas?"

Valentina's voice, a soft Southern twang and a little raspy —yes, even her voice dripped sex—punctured my train of thought.

"You didn't fall," I replied, belatedly answering her question. "I was right there, so I caught you."

Her nose wrinkled, and she lifted a hand, nervously twirling one of her curly locks around her fingers. "Oh," she said softly. She caught her bottom lip in her teeth, and I thought I just might not be able to manage myself around her.

I'd never been alone with her. That wasn't unusual. I was rarely alone with any woman. I had a six-year-old daughter who I was raising on my own, which didn't leave much time for anything. I had one priority, and that was Rylie, my little girl.

Usually, I wasn't even tempted. I was busy, fucking busy as hell. Between working as a first responder and working at the lodge and trying to be a parent, sometimes I wondered if I should schedule time to breathe. I didn't know what the hell I would do if my mom and sister weren't around to help me out with Rylie whenever I needed it.

To get to my point, I wasn't easily distracted. But Valentina, damn, the woman distracted me just by existing.

She eyed me warily, her cheeks still pink. "Well, thank you," she said politely. "I guess you saved me."

A grin twitched at the corners of my mouth again. In the past half an hour, with the exception of the time I spent with Rylie, I had smiled more than I had in years.

That was fucking depressing.

"I didn't really save you," I said. "I mean, you would've fallen and maybe sustained a bruise or two. But you'd have been fine. Always glad to help, though."

The temptation to lean forward and kiss her was so insanely strong that I had to force myself to stand abruptly. "Now that you're doing all right, I'll leave you be," I said, stepping back.

Valentina moved swiftly, swinging her legs off the bed and following me over to the door. It was then I realized I had dropped her package in the act of catching her. The vibrator had fallen out and lay on the floor in its molded plastic.

I might've sold my soul to see just what Valentina would be doing with it.

Incongruously, an open pocketknife and a Bible were on the floor as well. I gave my head a quick shake, uncertain what to think of the combination of a vibrator, a Bible, and a pocketknife. I couldn't quite sort out what Valentina had been doing before I arrived unless she had a habit of throwing random items on the floor.

She hurried past me, ignoring the Bible and knife, but picking up the vibrator and flinging it behind her onto the bed. As if we would somehow both forget it had ever been there.

The door to her cabin was still open, and I started to step through it. Just then, her hand caught my wrist. "Lucas," she said, her tone agitated.

With nothing more than the curl of her hand around my wrist, her touch felt like a ring of fire on my skin.

Turning back, I found her standing there, chewing on the bottom lip I wanted to kiss with her cheeks almost as red as her hair. "Yes?"

"Please don't mention this to anyone," she blurted out.

I shook my head. "Of course not. If your name had been on it, I wouldn't have opened it. Just so you know."

She nodded, her hand still around my wrist. "Right. It's just, I know how things get around. Wade's mother is friends with mine, and I might be twenty-five, but my parents still think I shouldn't even kiss a man unless I'm marrying him. I know that's weird, but I love them and ..." She paused to gulp in a breath.

It was downright crazy she thought I would mention this to anyone. I might keep to myself, but I wasn't an asshole. Not to mention, even if I told Wade, he would get a kick out of it, but he sure as hell would *not* tell his mother. As these thoughts passed through, Valentina kept on talking.

"You see, I don't have a boyfriend. I've never had a boyfriend. I wasn't allowed to have a boyfriend. And lately, well ..." She paused here to let out a ragged sigh. "I just thought I should do something about that. I mean it's embarrassing to be a virgin at my age, don't you think? It's just crazy." This time, her pause was nearly electric. "I'd appreciate it if you didn't tell anyone."

Valentina's light touch on my skin left my control

hanging by a thread. She was so damn honest it almost hurt, and there were not very many people like that in the world. I couldn't say I knew her well because she'd only started this job at the lodge a few months ago. Wade had mentioned in passing that she'd led a sheltered life and we should all be nice to her, or his mother would give him hell.

I wondered if he had any idea just *how* sheltered her life had been. So there was that, and the fact my brain was about to fucking explode with the knowledge that Valentina was a virgin.

———

Coming August 2019!
Wait For Me

If you love steamy, small town romance, take a visit to Willow Brook, Alaska in my Into The Fire Series. Check out Burn For Me - a second chance romance for the ages. It's FREE on all retailers! Don't miss Cade & Amelia's story!

Go here to sign up for information on new releases: http://jhcroixauthor.com/subscribe/

A NOTE ON SHAY'S STORY

In This Crazy Love, Shay faces painful challenges from her past on the way to her happily-ever-after. In writing her story, her destiny was in my hands, but we don't all get the ending we want. Many people move beyond terrible tragedies to heal and find happiness, and I believe it's so important to create hope by sharing those stories.

This is not the first time I've written about a character who experienced domestic violence. As I wrote Shay's story, I asked myself if I touch on the topic too often. Then, I realized it would be far less realistic if I didn't have characters with these experiences. Statistically speaking, that is.

As I have before, I'm including resources below. Finding help creates a path to the future. The strength of those who have moved beyond these situations is incredible.

Domestic violence is a social problem of massive proportions. It is estimated that approximately 20 people per minute experience physical abuse by an intimate partner in the United States, which translates to more than 10 million victims per year (National Coalition Against Domestic Violence, 2015). It is devastating and has life-long effects for victims, families and children touched by it. If you or anyone you know has experienced domestic violence (emotional, physical, psychological), there are resources for help.

The National Domestic Violence Hotline: http://www.thehotline.org

1-800-799-SAFE (7233)

National Coalition Against Domestic Violence: http://www.ncadv.org

Domesticshelters.org: https://www.domesticshelters.org

National Dating Abuse Hotline (for teens and youth): http://www.loveisrespect.org

1-866-331-9474

Americans Overseas Domestic Violence Crisis Center: www.866uswomen.org

International Toll-Free (24/7)

1-866-USWOMEN (879-6636)

National Child Abuse Hotline/Childhelp: www.childhelp.org

1-800-4-A-CHILD (1-800-422-4453)

National Sexual Assault Hotline: www.rainn.org

1-800-656-4673 (HOPE)

National Center for Victims of Crime: www.victimsofcrime.org

1-202-467-8700

Swoon Series

This Crazy Love

Wait For Me

Break My Fall

Into The Fire Series

Burn For Me

Slow Burn

Burn So Bad

Hot Mess

Burn So Good

Sweet Fire

Play With Fire

Melt With You

Burn For You

Crash & Burn

Brit Boys Sports Romance

The Play

Big Win

Out Of Bounds

Play Me

Naughty Wish

Diamond Creek Alaska Novels

When Love Comes

Follow Love

Love Unbroken

Love Untamed

Tumble Into Love

Christmas Nights

Last Frontier Lodge Novels

Take Me Home

Love at Last

Just This Once

Falling Fast

Stay With Me

When We Fall

Hold Me Close

ACKNOWLEDGMENTS

A shout out to my readers. If you made it to here, that's you! You keep reading my stories, cheering for my books & sending me messages when I need them most. Thank you for making it possible for me to keep writing.

Gracious thanks to my editor for not hesitating to tell me how to make every story better, and to Terri D. for proofreading like a champ.

To Janine, Beth P., Terri E., Heather H., & Carolyne B. Ya'll don't miss a detail!

Sometimes characters sneak into stories. I didn't plan ahead for Mischief to be in this story. He just butted his way into the very first scene. As inspiration goes, he was definitely inspired by a real horse.

I grew up riding horses. Most of my spare time in childhood all the way through high school was spent with horses. My mother also rode horses, and it was my job to feed the horses morning and evening and clean the stalls. So, yeah, I was busy. Since I rode the show circuit, this also meant hours upon hours of riding most days after school and on the weekends. I loved every minute.

I digress. My mother still has horses and ended up with a Banker pony when a rescue program was looking for someone to take care of a cute, impish pony. He's a bossy little guy and not even close to the size of her other horse, but he's in charge. His name isn't Mischief, but it would definitely fit.

I call more than one place home, but North Carolina is where I come from—I'll always be a Southern girl at heart. A bow of gratitude to the magical Blue Ridge Mountains.

Always, DBC & my dogs. You're there every day, in every way.

xoxo

J.H. Croix

ABOUT THE AUTHOR

USA Today Bestselling Author J. H. Croix lives in a small town in the historical farmlands of Maine with her husband and two spoiled dogs. Croix writes contemporary romance with sassy women and alpha men who aren't afraid to show some emotion. Her love for quirky small-towns and the characters that inhabit them shines through in her writing. Take a walk on the wild side of romance with her bestselling novels!

Places you can find me:
jhcroixauthor.com
jhcroix@jhcroix.com

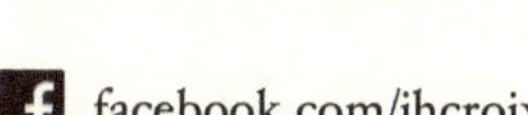 facebook.com/jhcroix

 twitter.com/jhcroix

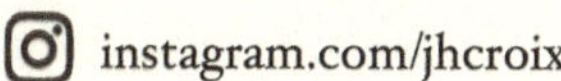 instagram.com/jhcroix

www.ingramcontent.com/pod-product-compliance
Lightning Source LLC
Chambersburg PA
CBHW050510190726
48284CB00003B/752